The Steps up
the Chimney

The Magician's House Quartet

The Steps up the Chimney
The Door in the Tree
The Tunnel behind the Waterfall
The Bridge in the Clouds

Also by William Corlett

Kitty
The Dark Side of the Moon

The Steps up the Chimney

Being the First Book of
The Magician's House

William Corlett

RED FOX

THE STEPS UP THE CHIMNEY
A RED FOX BOOK 0 099 48217 7

First published in Great Britain by The Bodley Head,
an imprint of Random House Children's Books

The Bodley Head edition published 1990
First Red Fox edition published 1991
Second Red Fox edition published 1999
This Red Fox edition published 2005

1 3 5 7 9 10 8 6 4 2

Papers used by Random House Children's Books are natural,
recyclable products made from wood grown in sustainable forests.
The manufacturing processes conform to the environmental
regulations of the country of origin.

Set in Sabon by Palimpsest Book Production Ltd,
Polmont, Stirlingshire

Red Fox Books are published by
Random House Children's Books,
61-63 Uxbridge Road, London W5 5SA,
a division of The Random House Group Ltd,
in Australia by Random House Australia (Pty) Ltd,
20 Alfred Street, Milsons Point, Sydney, NSW 2061, Australia,
in New Zealand by Random House New Zealand Ltd,
18 Poland Road, Glenfield, Auckland 10, New Zealand,
and in South Africa by Random House (Pty) Ltd,
Endulini, 5A Jubilee Road, Parktown 2193, South Africa

THE RANDOM HOUSE GROUP Limited Reg. No. 954009
www.kidsatrandomhouse.co.uk

A CIP catalogue record for this book is available from the British Library.

Printed and bound in Great Britain by
Bookmarque Ltd, Croydon, Surrey

Contents

1	At Druce Coven Halt	1
2	The Journey to Golden House	9
3	The First Night at Golden House	19
4	The Snow	29
5	The Conference	37
6	The Window	44
7	The Attic Rooms	55
8	Uncle Jack's Discoveries	66
9	Jonas Lewis's Book	74
10	When William Can't Sleep	83
11	Morning	94
12	The Dovecote	105
13	Tempers and Moods	120
14	The Steps up the Chimney	130
15	Meeting a Magician	140
16	Rats	156
17	Thoughts and Feathers	163
18	Christmas at Golden House	171
19	A Journey Through the Blizzard	184
20	Spot	197
21	A Day We'll Remember for the Rest of Our Lives	211
22	The Empty Room	227
23	The Return of the Magician	242
24	A Naming	256

For Bryn and The Dysons

1

At Druce Coven Halt

The station at Druce Coven was a lonely place. The line that served it was for most of its length a single track that wound through the bleak and lovely countryside of the Welsh and English borders from Manchester in the north to Bristol in the south. It meandered through desolate villages and deserted halts where sometimes only a thin strip of platform and a green painted hut indicated that here was indeed a stopping place.

William, who had taken the train from Manchester, was the first to arrive at Druce Coven. His sisters, Mary and Alice, coming from London, would change at Bristol and their train was expected ten minutes later. It had been arranged that Uncle Jack would meet them and drive them back to Golden House, a journey of some twenty miles. But when William alighted from the train, dragging his heavy suitcase after him, and slamming the door, he was surprised to find that he was alone on the platform. Uncle Jack hadn't arrived and no other passengers got off the train with him. There wasn't even a guard on the platform, nor a ticket office, because the train was more like a bus and fares were paid to the conductor on board. For a moment he wondered if he was in fact in the right place. Leaving his case he walked towards the fence, where a gate swung and creaked in the wind. Beside the gate, a long sign with white letters painted on peeling green proclaimed that this was DRUCE COVEN HALT. That was where he had been told to expect his uncle. At least, he thought, I'm here first. Mary and Alice wouldn't have liked it, being younger. And, he had to admit, it was a lonely place even for him. He shivered and looked round apprehensively.

It was a cold, dull December afternoon. The rain that had been threatening all day pressed heavily on the swollen clouds. A thin wind moaned through the struts of the fence and tugged at a loose board on the roof of the seat shelter. The halt was situated in a deep cutting, so that it wasn't possible to see the country that surrounded it. A bridge crossed the cutting. Ahead of him, towards Bristol, the line disappeared into a dark tunnel.

William stuffed his hands into the pockets of his anorak and kicked a stone. It skidded and clattered against the opposite side of the track, where the steep bank was over-grown with weeds and stunted shrubs and trees. He walked a few steps along the platform, then turned and walked the same number back. Then he looked at his watch. The Bristol train was due in eight minutes. He retraced his steps to his suitcase and sat down.

At the top of the bank opposite to him, a thick belt of trees crowded up to a solid wooden fence. As he looked at them, a fox suddenly broke cover and stood, with one front paw raised, looking down into the cutting. The brilliant red of its coat seemed almost to flash with light against the dull surroundings. William leaned forward, surprised and excited by its unexpected appearance. As he did so, the animal turned its head and stared at him. It seemed to William as if the fox's eyes were in a direct line with his own; as though for a moment, they were both of them held by some invisible string.

'Hello there!' a voice called, breaking the unnatural stillness in the narrow cutting.

So surprising and unexpected was the voice that it seemed almost as if it had been the fox who had spoken, but William knew that was ridiculous. Still it remained staring at him for a moment longer then, as silently and stealthily as it had arrived, it disappeared once more into the undergrowth.

William shivered and blinked. He felt cold and disappointed. He had liked the fox. It had been almost a friend on the desolate platform. Now that it was gone, he missed its company.

'You boy. Hello!' the voice called again, bringing William back to the present. Turning, he saw a man leaning over the bridge, looking down at him. Once again eyes searched out his own; once again the invisible string seemed to connect William to the man who was now looking at him. The eyes of the man, like the eyes of the fox, seemed to probe into William's mind, as though they were searching his thoughts. He tried to look away but he was unable to do so, so powerful seemed the gaze.

'Lost your tongue, boy?' the man called.

'No,' William replied, his voice coming out almost defiantly, but, as he spoke, he stood up. He felt a surge of panic, and glanced nervously over his shoulder, as if searching for somewhere to hide.

'I'm sorry,' the man said more gently. 'I startled you. But, surely – aren't you expecting someone to meet you here?'

'My uncle,' William replied.

'Ah, yes. That's right. But – you're alone?'

'My sisters are coming from London. They'll be on the next train.' Although the man asked such direct questions and although his eyes continued to stare so deeply into William's, he didn't seem altogether unfriendly.

'Stay there,' he now said, and a moment later William saw him walking down the short, steep track to the gate in the fence and out on to the platform in front of him.

'What's your name, boy?' the man asked.

'William. William Constant.'

'William Constant,' the man repeated quietly, and

4

then he smiled and was silent. He was tall and thin, with a high forehead and receding hair. His eyes were very pale; blue-grey and flecked with gold that seemed almost to sparkle. His hair, what was left of it, was wispy and long; the wind blew it in a haze of red round his head, like a cloud. He was wearing a long black mac, buttoned to the chin.

'Well, William Constant,' he said at last, 'you're the oldest, are you?'

'Yes. I'm thirteen.'

'And the others? Your sisters?'

'Mary is eleven and Alice is eight.'

The man nodded, a slow, deliberate movement of the head.

'And you're going to stay at the Golden House, am I right?'

'My uncle lives there. D'you know him?'

'I've seen him, yes. And his wife. It is his wife, is it?'

'Phoebe. That's her name.'

'His wife?'

'Sort of,' William replied reluctantly. He did feel a bit nervous under the penetrating gaze and, although he didn't at all like this cross-examination, he found it difficult not to answer the man's questions.

'There's no need to be afraid, William. I mean you no harm,' the man told him, and reaching out, he put a hand lightly on William's shoulder.

'I'm not afraid,' William protested defiantly, but really he wished that he wasn't all alone with this man who stared so searchingly into his eyes as the fox had done.

'Is it the first fox you've seen?' the man asked, seeming to read his thoughts.

'Well, I've seen them on television of course. But I've never seen one in the wild before.'

'There are badgers at the Golden House and otters in the river. You'll see them, as well, I dare say.'

'Do you live near here then?'

'I know the area,' the man replied quietly and as he did so, his face looked sad.

'We're staying there for the Christmas holidays. Our parents are working abroad. They're both doctors. They're out in Ethiopia, working in a hospital. Well, it's more of a camp really . . .' William knew that he was suddenly speaking too much and too fast, but the man's sad expression made him want to fill in the silences.

The man's hand was still resting on his shoulder. It felt heavy and now it gripped at William's anorak, so that he was pulled towards him.

Distantly, behind him, William heard the long, plaintive whistle of an approaching train.

'Here's the train,' he said, without looking round. 'You'll be able to meet Mary and Alice. What's your name, by the way? So that I can introduce you?'

The man clung to his shoulder, staring into his eyes.

'My name is Stephen Tyler, William. Will you remember that?'

Much nearer now the whistle sounded again. William turned and saw the diesel train come out of the gloom of the tunnel towards him. With a hiss and a shudder it came to a halt. For a moment nothing happened, then one of the windows opened and a girl with short brown hair stuck her head out.

'William,' she called, 'can you help? The door's stuck.'

William hurried along the short platform and opened the door for her. The girl climbed out and turned back to drag down her suitcase.

'Here, Mary, I'll do that,' William said, trying to push past her.

'I can manage,' his sister retorted, pulling at the heavy case.

'Will. Help me instead,' Alice, his younger sister called, appearing at the open doorway. 'Only hurry, or the train'll start again.'

As William lifted Alice's suitcase down on to the platform he glanced back to where Mr Tyler was still standing, watching the arrival. Then William swung round and taking Alice's hands, he helped her to jump down on to the platform.

As soon as he slammed the door, the train started to move off. Alice held on to William's hands for an instant, then jumped up and gave him a kiss.

'Don't be soppy, Alice,' he protested. Then he remembered Mr Tyler. 'This man knows Golden House quite well,' he said and he turned to introduce his sisters.

'What man?' Mary demanded.

The platform was empty.

'How funny. There was a man here . . . You must have seen him. I was standing with him, when you called to me from the train. Where's he gone?'

'I didn't see anyone,' Mary said, bending to pick up her suitcase.

'But he was here.'

'Well he isn't here now, is he?'

'But – where did he go?'

'I don't know,' Mary said, with an unhelpful shrug. 'Oh, this suitcase weighs a ton.'

'Maybe he got on the train, Will,' Alice said as she also picked up her case.

'I suppose so,' William said, still puzzled by the man's sudden disappearance.

'There's Uncle Jack,' Alice squealed and, dropping her case once more, she ran along the platform to where a man wearing jeans and a sweater was hurrying down the track towards the gate.

'Sorry I'm late!' he was calling. 'I got held up by some sheep.'

2

The Journey to Golden House

Jack's ancient Land-Rover was parked at the top of the track on the narrow lane that crossed the railway by the bridge and then disappeared in amongst trees in both directions.

'It's all part of an ancient forest,' Jack explained as he carried the girls' cases and put them in the back of the motor. 'At one time it stretched as far as the Forest of Dean in the south. But of course, over the centuries, much of it has been felled.'

'The Royal Forest of Dean,' Mary corrected him. 'That's where Nelson got all the oak for his ships from. We did it in history.'

'Oh, Mary!' her sister said, climbing up on to the front seat, beside the driver. 'The last thing we want to hear is one of your history lessons. They're so boring.'

'Alice! I want to sit in the front,' William said, putting his case in the back and walking round to stand beside her.

'No. I got here first.'

'They're always squabbling,' Mary confided to Jack. 'And that's really boring.'

'William, get off me!' Alice yelled, as her brother sat firmly on top of her.

'Get off her, William. You can both sit in the back,' Jack told them.

'I want to sit in the front beside you,' Alice wailed.

'Well, you can't. Go on, Mary, you sit in front,' Jack said, climbing into the driver's seat.

'But why?' Alice protested.

'Because she waited,' Jack told her.

After some more arguing William and Alice climbed into the back and Mary sat beside Jack. As she did so, she glanced at him and smiled. Then she ran her hand through her hair.

'I'm growing my hair. It used to be quite short. Do you like it?'

'Ugh! Stop flirting, Mary,' Alice said. 'Be careful, Uncle Jack. She's man mad!' and she started to giggle.

'Honestly, you're such a baby, Alice,' Mary said and she looked out of the window to hide the fact that she was blushing.

'You're blushing,' Alice sang the words. 'Mary's blushing.'

'Shut up, Alice!' Mary said, sounding really cross.

'Yes! Shut up, Alice,' Jack rejoined. But he looked over his shoulder and smiled at her as he spoke.

Alice shrugged and pouted. She was outnumbered and it wasn't fair. She swung her legs and looked at the floor. An uneasy silence followed.

'D'you know what, Uncle Jack, I saw a fox. When I was waiting at the station,' William said, remembering again the sharp, enquiring eyes.

'There are a lot of them round here. We have one at the house. It comes into the garden at night. You don't often see them during the day though.'

'And there are badgers, aren't there? And otters in the river,' William continued, enthusiastically.

'Who told you all that?'

'The man.'

'What man?' his uncle asked, glancing at William in the driving mirror.

'Will has a mysterious man, who wasn't there,' Mary volunteered, tucking her legs up under her and swinging round on the seat so that she was resting her hands on the back of it.

'He got on the train, Mary. We worked that out,' Alice told her, spitefully.

'He was there,' William protested. 'I spent ages talking to him. His name was Stephen Tyler.'

Jack glanced at his nephew again in the driving mirror.

'Stephen who?' he asked.

'No, Doctor Who!' Alice corrected and giggled again.

'Tyler,' William repeated. 'He said I was to remember the name.'

'Well, it isn't a very difficult one, is it?' Mary said. 'Not like Alicia Borodevski.'

'Alicia . . . who?' Jack laughed.

'Borodevski,' Mary repeated, pleased with the effect she had made. 'She's a girl in our class. Her great-grandfather was a white Russian.'

'Aren't they all white?' Alice asked.

'I don't know,' Mary retorted. 'But she's one. Her family can never go back to Moscow in case they get put in prison. That's what she said, anyway. They were all friends of the Tsar. And they ran away with jewels sewed into their linings . . .'

'That's the story of that film with that bald actor,' William said, scathingly. 'Honestly, Mare, you'd believe anything. Anyway, Mr Tyler said there were otters and badgers at Golden House.'

'Well, I've never seen any otters. I think there are badgers. How did this man know so much about Golden House anyway?'

'Maybe he used to live there,' Mary said.

'No. It's been empty for years. And the last owner was an old lady called Miss Crawden and she'd lived there for ages with her family and then on her own, I think.'

'Anyway, he didn't live there,' William cut in. 'He just said that he knew the area.'

'We haven't got to know anyone yet,' Jack said. 'I expect there are lots of cottages tucked away in the hills.'

The conversation in the van came to an end and the children stared out of the windows at the moving scene. The light was beginning to fade and a fine rain was falling. The road wound through the forest and then suddenly out into rural countryside, with hedgerows in place of the dense overgrowth of the trees. They were in a narrow valley, the fields rising sharply on either side of the lane which climbed steeply ahead of them. Reaching the top of this hill, Jack stopped driving for a moment so that they could look at the view. In front of them, pale and grey against the darkening sky, a long range of rolling moorland was revealed, with the peaks of higher mountains beyond.

'That's Wales, over there. Welsh Wales, they call it. And this is English Wales, I suppose. We're nearly home,' Jack told them and a little later, he turned the Land-Rover off the road into an even narrower track that wound ahead of them up over the side of the valley. The hedgerows disappeared and they were soon on the side of an open moor.

'This road'll get pretty bad, come the snow,' Jack said, almost as if he was talking to himself. 'If it closes, we'll be cut off.'

'I hope it happens while we're here,' Alice told him, 'then we wouldn't have to go back to school.'

'I thought you liked school,' Jack said, concentrating on the road ahead.

'I do,' Alice replied and lapsed into silence once more.

The light was fading fast and had reached that uncomfortable gloaming where nothing is quite distinguishable. Jack switched on the headlights. As he did so, a bright streak of red dashed across the road ahead of them, making him brake suddenly.

'Did you see that?' he asked, with surprise. 'A fox. I nearly ran into it.'

'I saw it,' Mary cried.

'And I did,' Alice added excitedly. 'Did you, Will? Did you see it?'

But William remained silent, staring out into the thin light, transfixed by the two bright eyes that stared at him from the secret depths of the ditch at the road's side. And, as the motor started up once more and the Land-Rover moved forward, so he swivelled round until he was looking out of the back window, unable to break the invisible string that seemed to attach him to them.

'Are we nearly there?' Alice asked later, breaking the renewed silence. 'I'm starving.'

'Not much further. The road drops down again and then we turn into Golden Valley.'

It was already dark when they reached the valley. The rain had stopped and a wind was rattling the branches of the trees. The road was climbing steeply again and there was the sound of running water.

'The brook follows the track all along here,' Jack explained. 'It's a pity it's dark. But you'll see it all tomorrow. Listen,' and an owl hooted somewhere near by.

'Why is it called Golden Valley, Uncle Jack?' Mary asked.

'I haven't a clue,' he replied. 'There's another Golden Valley over towards Hereford as well. Maybe ours was named after the house – or was the house named after the valley? I don't know.'

'Maybe they dug for gold here,' Alice suggested, excited by the idea. But Jack told her he thought it unlikely.

'Is all this your land?' Mary asked, staring out of the window.

'No. It probably was once. But now it belongs to the local landlord. We just have two acres.'

'Will we be allowed to explore it, seeing it doesn't belong to you?' she asked.

'I expect so. There are lots of footpaths. I've got an Ordnance Survey map at the house. Just don't go causing any trouble, though. I want to keep in with the natives! We're here,' and, as he spoke, ahead of them a light glimmered distantly through the trees. He slowed the motor once more in front of a gate. 'William, can you hop out and open the gate, please?'

The night air was cold after the enclosed atmosphere.

William walked in the light of the headlamps towards the wooden gate and swung it open. As he waited for the Land-Rover to drive through he looked round at the dense trees that reared up on either side of the valley. The wind was loud in the branches and the sound of the brook was overpowering. Then another sound, a soft panting, snuffling, breathing sort of sound, made him look behind him, searching in the darkness for its source. Although he couldn't see anything, he had a strange and eerie sense that he was being watched.

'Go away,' he whispered and he noticed that his voice was shaking with fear.

'Hey – William! Hurry up!' Jack called and William swung the gate closed and scrambled back into the safety of the Land-Rover.

'Brrrh!' Jack said, driving on. 'It's cold enough for snow.'

By the time they arrived at the house the night was completely dark and it was impossible to see anything except the vaguest outline. A light was burning in the porch and there was an impression of a sprawling building with many darkened windows.

'Welcome to Golden House,' Jack said and a moment later, as the motor came to a halt, the front door opened and a young woman appeared, her silhouette framed in the light from the hall behind her. Her pale-blonde hair hung in a sheet down her back and stirred in the breeze as she moved. She was wearing a long, loose-fitting garment which failed to hide an enlarged stomach.

'Uncle Jack!' Mary exclaimed before she could stop herself. 'Phoebe's pregnant!'

'Yes,' he replied, 'didn't I tell you?' and then the figure ran out of the door towards them, her arms extended in greeting.

'Here you are,' she said. 'Supper's all ready. You must be starving.' As she spoke she put her arms round Jack's neck and kissed him on the cheek.

'Everything OK?' he asked her. She nodded and smiled.

'I'm not used to being on my own here yet,' she explained shyly to the children. 'But, all the same, he worries too much. Now, let me see you. Goodness! You've all grown so much. Come inside, quickly. It's freezing out here,' and she hurried them into the house leaving Jack to bring the cases.

'I'll help you, Uncle Jack,' William said, turning at the doorway and going back to where he was struggling with all three cases at the same time.

'Thanks. You all right?'

'Yes,' William replied, avoiding his uncle's eyes.

'You seemed a bit quiet on the journey.'

'I'm all right, honestly I am,' the boy said and taking one of the cases he went into the house.

As Jack followed him in and closed the front door, the moon came out from behind the clouds and cast pale shadows amongst the trees and across the rough grass that skirted the drive. An owl hooted at a distance and, nearer, a strange staccato barking indicated the whereabouts of the fox.

3

The First Night at Golden House

Jack and Phoebe had only been at Golden House for a few months and most of the building was still in a terrible state of disrepair. They had, however, made comfortable a section of the centre, around the main hall, and it was here that they intended to live while Jack gradually renovated the rest. The idea was that eventually they would open the house as a hotel.

The hall that the children entered was the oldest part of the building and dated back to the Middle Ages. It had a stone-flagged floor and a huge fireplace that had been put in during Tudor times, Jack explained to them.

'Before that there would just have been a hole in the roof,' he said.

A staircase rose from the hall to a gallery that ran round three sides, with doors leading into the various upper rooms. One was Jack and Phoebe's bedroom, a second was a huge and antiquated bathroom. All the others were in varying states of chaos. Building materials and paints in one, furniture piled high in another, cobwebs and fallen plaster and the grime and dust of the years in the others.

A second staircase, narrow and spiralling, behind a door in one corner of the gallery led up to three smaller, low-ceilinged attics, with exposed beams that crossed the rooms like horizontal bars in a gymnasium. Two of these rooms had been prepared for the children. Mary and Alice were to share one and William had the second one to himself. Up here there was also a bathroom and lavatory that had obviously been recently installed.

'Specially for your visit,' Jack said, with a note of pride in his voice. Then he grinned. 'I hope it all works. I've never actually done plumbing before.'

The rooms had been painted and there were new curtains at the small dormer windows and matching bedspreads on the single beds. The wooden floors had old rugs on them and there were lamps beside each of the beds.

'Why don't we ever get rooms of our own?' Mary demanded crossly. 'William always does. Just because he's a boy. It isn't fair.'

'I don't mind sharing with you, Mare,' Alice said in a small voice.

'That's not the point. I mind sharing with you. I want a room to myself.'

'It's ever such a big house, Mare,' Alice whispered, her eyes wide as she looked round at all the dark corners on the landing outside their door.

'You're such a wimp, Alice,' Mary said and then she screamed and dived for her bed, as William jumped out of his room with a snarl.

'William! I'll kill you if you do that again. I swear I will.'

'Don't, Will,' Alice said, still using her 'small' voice. 'I don't like it here.'

William put an arm round her and hugged her.

'It's all right, Al. I'll be next door. And Uncle Jack's just downstairs.'

'But what if a witch comes in the night?' Mary whispered, warming to her subject. 'You wouldn't hear us if she put a spell on us straight away. She could take us off into one of the other rooms, where Uncle Jack hasn't even been yet, and she could lock us away and make us sleep for ever and no one would even know where to look for us.'

Alice sat on the edge of her bed, wide-eyed and hugging herself. As Mary finished speaking she suddenly leaped across the room, wailing and waving her hands in front of her. Alice shot back up the bed and pulled the eiderdown over her head.

'Mary,' William said, using his big brother voice, 'you're scaring Alice.'

'No she isn't. I think she's stupid,' Alice said, her head still under the eiderdown.

'And the witch would come each day and fatten you up,' Mary continued, kneeling on the bed in front of the crouched figure under the eiderdown. 'And she'd come and prod you every so often to see if you were ready to EAT!' As she shouted the word eat, her hands dived under the eiderdown and she started to tickle her sister.

'Stop it, Mary. Stop it!' Alice pleaded, shrieking and giggling helplessly at the same time.

'Mary, I'm warning you!' William said and he dived on top of her, pulling her off Alice.

This unexpected onslaught knocked Mary off balance and she started to topple off the bed. Grabbing Alice, she tried to steady herself, but instead all three of them landed on the floor with a bump and lay there panting and exhausted.

'Ugh. I feel sick now,' Alice groaned, and she started to laugh again.

'Hey, you lot!' they heard Jack calling up the staircase from the gallery below. 'Supper.'

'Ugh! Supper! I'll be sick,' Alice moaned, then she got to her feet and ran for the door. 'Mary doesn't want any supper, Uncle Jack. She's lying down,' she yelled.

'You liar, Alice!' Mary said, scrambling to her feet just as Jack came into the room.

'What's going on?' he asked, anxiously. 'Are you ill?'

'Take no notice of them,' William confided in him. 'They're all right really.'

'She was lying down,' Alice said.

'Little things please little minds, Alice,' Mary said, tucking her blouse into her waistband. But Alice had already left the room and was clattering down the stone stairs.

The table was laid in the kitchen, a large room situated at the back of the house through a door from the hall. It had an old cast-iron kitchen range, in which a fire glowed. Two wooden-backed armchairs stood on either side of the hearth, with bright cushions on their seats. There was a dresser, its shelves crowded with crockery, and cupboards for the pots and pans. Along one wall a stone trough served as a sink and beside it there was a cold water pump. An old-fashioned, electric water heater was fixed to the wall beside it, with a pipe leading from the pump. In the wall behind the sink, a long, low window looked out into the dark night.

'We meant to have so much finished before you arrived,' Phoebe apologized, 'including curtains in here. Sorry! But there's always so much to do. Now, Mary, if you sit there, with William beside you and Alice here, beside me.'

As she spoke she brought a soup tureen to the table and started to ladle out bowls of steaming broth. Jack meanwhile was cutting a loaf of brown bread.

'What's your favourite food?' Phoebe asked.

'Sausages and baked beans,' Alice replied at once.

'Hamburgers,' William and Mary chorused in unison.

'Oh dear,' Phoebe exclaimed. 'I'm afraid you're going to hate it here.'

'We're vegetarians,' Jack explained.

'Doesn't matter,' Mary said after a moment, feeling that someone should speak.

'What's a vegetarian?' Alice asked.

'What d'you think, idiot,' William said, looking distinctly embarrassed.

'I don't know, do I? That's why I asked.'

'They just eat vegetables,' William said in a half whisper, as though hoping that he wouldn't be heard.

'Ugh!' Alice shrieked. 'But I hate vegetables!'

'We do eat other things,' Jack said with a laugh. 'Rice and lentils and cheese and . . .'

'Delicious soup, Aunt Phoebe . . . I mean . . . Phoebe,' Mary said, trying to ease the situation and making it worse with her mistake. Then she blushed.

'You can call me Aunt Phoebe, if you want to,' Phoebe said, smiling.

'But you're not, are you?' Alice interjected, blowing on a spoonful of hot soup. 'You'd have to be married to Uncle Jack in order to be our aunt, wouldn't you?'

'I suppose so,' Phoebe replied and she glanced at Jack, as if looking for support.

'When's the baby expected?' Mary asked, trying once again to make polite conversation.

'At the end of January,' Phoebe replied.

'But . . .' Alice couldn't stop herself saying, although William was staring at her dangerously. She closed her mouth, willing herself not to speak any more.

'But what, Alice?' Phoebe asked.

'Nothing,' she mumbled.

The soup was followed by macaroni cheese, with jacket potatoes and salad, and the rest of the meal passed without too many awkward moments except when William asked if there was any ketchup.

'Oh dear. There's some home-made chutney, would that do?' Phoebe asked, hopefully.

'It doesn't matter,' William told her and wished that the ground would swallow him up.

'It's quite nice, Will,' Alice told him, tucking into her plateful and wanting to be reassuring.

'I love jacket potatoes,' Mary said, valiantly.

However, the pudding, it was agreed all round, was 'brill'. Mary said so and Alice said so and William nodded and asked for a second helping. It was a treacle and banana tart and Phoebe said she'd made up the recipe.

'She's really great at puddings,' Jack said, helping himself to another portion. 'You wait till you taste her chocolate mousse.'

'Did you notice?' Mary said when the girls were in bed and William was sitting on the floor between them wrapped in the eiderdown from his own room. 'He's obviously madly in love with her.'

'Ugh! How revolting,' Alice protested.

'How was it obvious?' William said. 'I don't think it was obvious at all.'

'Women notice these things,' Mary told him smugly.

'You're not a woman, Mary,' Alice rounded on her, impatiently, 'and anyway, if they're so in love – why don't they get married? William – what'll happen to the baby, if they're not?'

'Nothing,' William replied. 'It won't make any difference'.

'Except – it'll be born out of wedlock,' Mary said in a dramatic whisper.

'What's wedlock?' Alice asked, nervously. It sounded pretty gruesome.

'Being married, that's all. Don't listen to Mary, she's in one of her funny moods. You don't have to be married to have babies,' William told her.

'I know that,' Alice wailed, in an exasperated voice. 'But all the same . . . well, I mean, if it doesn't matter, then why does anyone get married?'

The three of them considered this for a moment.

'I used to think you had to be married to have babies,' Mary then said.

'You don't though, do you?' Alice asked uncertainly.

'No. Of course you don't.'

'That's what I just said, Mary. Don't be such a know-all.'

'Shut up squabbling, you two,' William interrupted them. 'Of course you don't have to be married to have babies. But in the old days it was a sin if you weren't. Only now people don't believe that so much. Or, at least, some do and some don't.'

'Isn't it confusing?' Alice sighed.

'All the same,' Mary said thoughtfully, 'I wonder why they haven't got married.'

'Ask them,' William said, trying to end the discussion.

'I couldn't,' Mary protested. 'I'd be embarrassed.'

'I will. I don't mind,' Alice said.

'No, Alice. Just leave it,' her brother advised her. 'Anyway, Mum said they were going to get married eventually.'

'But that was ages ago, and they still haven't.'

'Maybe they want to get the house right first,' William suggested, without much conviction.

'But that'll take for ever and the baby will be out of wedlock.' Alice started to sob, dramatically, and then she yawned noisily.

'I'm going to bed,' William said, getting up and crossing to the door. 'It's freezing in here.'

'It's lovely and warm in bed,' Mary said, drowsily. 'Good night, Will.'

'Night Mare!' William said with mock terror, cracking one of their oldest jokes. 'Night, Al.' But Alice was already asleep. He switched off both the lamps and tiptoed to the door.

The landing was in darkness, as he crossed to his own door, but thin moonlight filled his room with an eerie white haze. He went to the little window and looked out into the night. At first he could see nothing, but gradually, as his eyes grew accustomed to the half-dark he saw the steeply pitched tiled roof of the house and below it a corner of the moonlit garden. Further off, a bank of wind-tossed trees rose towards a starry sky. Clouds moved fast across an almost full moon, which shone down from somewhere so near above him that he felt as if he could open the window and reach out and touch it. Then, as he was about to leave the window and go to his bed, a dark shape fluttered into view in front of him, making him pull back, startled and for a moment afraid. The shape came to rest out on the sloping roof just below the window. After a moment's fearful confusion, he realized that it was a great, dark bird. It folded its wings close to its body and then slowly turned its head, as though on a pivot. Two huge, white-ringed eyes stared at him and blinked. William remained poised and breathlessly watching until the owl, with a long, sad, ghostly sound, half flute-whistle, half human sigh, turned its head once more and, stretching its wings, floated away on the moonlit air out of his sight.

4

The Snow

Mary woke with a start. The room was unfamiliar and it took her a moment to remember where she was. The light was very bright. She sat up and, as the bed covers fell from her shoulders, she shivered. It was terribly cold. Then she saw Alice kneeling at the window, covered by an eiderdown.

'Alice? What are you doing? You'll freeze to death.'

Her younger sister looked round at her and smiled.

'Come and see,' she whispered, beckoning her to the window.

Mary pulled her eiderdown off the bed to cover herself and skipped across the cold floor to the window.

Outside the window a pale lemon-coloured sun shone from a hazy sky. All the land beneath it was white. The sloping tiles were white. The trees were white. Long icicles hung from the gutter at the side of the window, glittering in the light, and a gentle breeze blew fine white clouds across the surface of the roof.

'Snow,' Mary whispered.

'Isn't it beautiful, Mare?' Alice murmured.

'It's cold,' Mary said, scuttling back to the warmth of her bed.

'I'm going to see if William's awake,' Alice said and she ran from the room.

But William was not only asleep, he was also reluctant to be woken. Alice shook him a few times and tried to excite him with the prospect of the snow. But he only told her to: 'Gerroff, Alice!' and put his head under the covers.

Disappointed, she returned to her room and finding Mary also snuggled up and with her eyes closed she went and stared glumly out of the window again.

The whiteness of the view was almost blinding and Alice had to wrinkle up the corners of her eyes to shut out some of the dazzle. Her breath had steamed up the window. She rubbed at it with the palm of her hand, clearing a small patch. As she did so, a movement in the trees at the edge of the drive, part of which was just visible to her, attracted her attention. Kneeling up and craning sideways Alice could see a set of footprints in the deep snow. They led from the drive into the wood and then disappeared from view. Although she couldn't now see who had made them, she was certain that whoever it was had been there a moment before.

'Mary,' she said, 'there's someone out there.'

But Mary was asleep. With an impatient shrug, Alice started to dress. She pulled on her jeans and a thick jumper, a pair of socks and a knitted hat. She couldn't find her gloves and she realized that she hadn't brought her wellingtons, but her trainers were under the bed where she had left them the night before. Picking them up, she ran quickly out of the room and down the spiral staircase.

The hall was in gloomy shadows. Alice paused briefly to put on her shoes, then she crossed to open the great oak front door. It was locked, but the key was still there. It took all her strength and both her hands to turn it and even then the door wouldn't budge. She realized that it was bolted, top and bottom. The bottom bolt was easy enough for her to deal with. But in order to reach the top one, she had to drag a wooden chair across to stand on. Eventually, the door was unlocked and, tugging at it while turning the iron handle, Alice swung it open and stepped out into the frosty, sparkling air.

It was a silent, crisp world she entered. Her breath smoked in front of her and the cold tingled her cheeks. The snow stretched in a perfect, unblemished carpet as far as the edge of the wood. The drive led off to the right and, at a distance along it, she could just see the dark patches of the footprints that she had first noticed from the bedroom window.

Stepping out of the porch, Alice placed her foot lightly on the surface of the snow. It squeaked as her weight sank into it. Then she took another step, followed by another and then another. Each time her foot made the same crunching, squeaking sound as the fresh snow was broken. It was like being an explorer in an unknown land, or the first astronaut setting foot on the moon. Each step was so entirely new.

When she reached the place where the footprints left the drive she paused. For the first time she wondered who it could be who had made them. And then it occurred to her that whoever it was hadn't come from the direction of the house. Perhaps vaguely she'd thought that it could have been Uncle Jack, out for an early walk, but now that she was down at ground level, she could see quite clearly that the trail of prints came from along the drive in the opposite direction. This fact struck her as somehow odd and made her hesitate before dashing off in pursuit of the unknown person. She stood on the edge of the drive, scanning the dense trees, hoping that she could perhaps see something without having to venture too far into the woods. The silence was immense. The snow muffled everything. Even her own breathing sounded removed and distant.

'Hello,' she called, in a small voice. 'Hello. Anybody there?' But no answering sound or call came back to her. Lifting her foot, she placed it in the footprint in front of her. It was bigger than hers and the stretch to the next step was far greater than she could manage comfortably.

'Hello,' she called again. She reached forward and placed her second foot in the next printmark. Her stride was now so long that she nearly fell over trying to lift her first foot out of the snow. 'Oh, this is silly!' she said out loud, and she ran quickly towards the wood, following the footprints.

The wind had blown the snow in a slant under the trees and it was possible to follow the prints for quite a distance. They went in a more-or-less straight line, dodging round trees and following a steep uphill course until they reached an open clearing.

Halfway across this clearing, to Alice's surprise, they came to an abrupt end. For half the length of the clearing, there were distinct footprints and then . . . they disappeared. Alice stood at the spot where they vanished and stared at the snow. It wasn't possible. Where had they gone? She searched the ground ahead to see if in some way they had been obliterated and were once more in evidence further on. But there was no more sign of them. In fact a little further across the clearing the snow was all disturbed, as though an animal had been there, and also there were a lot of bird prints, but the human footsteps came to an abrupt end.

As the significance of this discovery slowly dawned on her, Alice looked round nervously. Below her the trees grew so close together that she could see neither the house nor the drive. In fact she'd climbed so high that she was able to look across the valley to its other side. There the trees were less snow covered. They stood, gaunt and dark against the white land, like a charcoal drawing. Above and beyond them, the vague outline of higher mountains blended into the thin haze. A wind was blowing, bringing dark clouds that rolled in over the valley and across the sky until the sun was hidden. It suddenly turned much colder. Then, somewhere near to her an animal howled. The sound, long and echoing, was strange and ghostly.

Alice at once turned and started to run as fast as she could back down the slope in the direction of the drive. She willed herself not to turn round, convinced that whatever the animal, be it wolf or mad dog or who knew what other frightening creature, it was just behind her and at any minute would pounce on her, tearing at her skin with its claws and snapping with its teeth.

She reached the tree line and slid and slipped her way down through the wood, then, just as she caught sight of the driveway, her foot went under a root and she tripped and fell headlong down the last bit of the hill and rolled out on to the thick snow at the bottom.

She lay, panting and dazed. But a moment later it seemed as though her fears were justified. A big black and white dog bounded out of the trees and raced round her, barking and jumping. Alice remained crouched on the ground, trembling with fear. But the dog didn't attack her. It kept springing round her, tail wagging, front paws burrowing into the snow, tongue licking the air.

'Good dog,' Alice whispered, uncertainly, trying to be brave.

At the sound of her voice the dog whimpered delightedly, and dodged forward, snapping at the air. Then, sitting on the snow in front of her, it raised a paw, as if wanting to shake hands.

'Good dog,' Alice said again, this time a little louder. And she also held out her hand to let the animal have a sniff.

The dog licked her hand and scrambled forward, whimpering excitedly. Alice stood up. The dog also rose and stood beside her, looking up at her, as if waiting for a command.

'I've got to go home now,' she said and she started to run towards the house. When she reached the porch, she looked back. The dog was still standing where she had left it, one paw raised off the ground, its head erect, watching her.

'Goodbye,' she called and at once the dog turned and raced off up the steep side of the valley into the trees.

'Alice, where have you been? We've been searching everywhere,' William said as she entered the hall. He was halfway down the stairs and looked as if he was going to be cross.

'Oh, Will,' Alice said and she ran to him and put her arms round him.

'Get off,' he said. 'You're soaking. What have you been doing?'

'I went out in the snow,' she said and hurried past him up the stairs.

'Now where are you going?'

'To change,' she replied in a sulky voice. 'You just said I'm soaking.'

'Well hurry up. Breakfast's ready – and don't you dare ask for bacon!' he said threateningly, as he went down the last of the stairs and towards the kitchen door.

'Will,' Alice called, stopping at the gallery and leaning over the banister.

'What?' William asked, stopping also and looking up at her.

'There's something ever so strange about this place,' she said.

'I know,' William said, quietly.

'You think so too?' Alice said, surprised by his agreement.

'We'll have a conference after breakfast,' he said and went through the kitchen door.

5

The Conference

'Well, I think you're making a lot of fuss about nothing,' Mary said, staring at herself in the mirror and brushing her hair over her forehead to see if a fringe suited her.

'Just because nothing's happened to you yet,' William said. 'Honestly, Mary. You're impossible sometimes. And stop staring at yourself in the mirror. It's vain.'

'I'm doing my hair. And anyway I'm so beautiful I can't stop looking at myself!' She grinned and stuck her tongue out at her brother and sister.

They were in the girls' room having the conference that William had suggested before breakfast. It was now the middle of the morning, but it was so dark in the room that the bedside lamps were switched on. Outside, the sky was covered with cloud, as more snow threatened.

'Anyway,' Alice protested, 'I could take you to where the footprints disappear. I could show you.'

'So?' Mary said. 'It doesn't prove anything. There could have been an avalanche that covered the rest of them . . .'

'Don't be stupid, Mary. We're not in Switzerland.'

'Well, there's snow, isn't there? And Alice said it was steep. The snow could have slid . . . that's all an avalanche is.'

'But it didn't, Mary. It was all smooth. Oh, please let me show you . . .'

'I believe you, Alice,' William said, getting up and crossing to the window. 'But, if we don't go soon, the footprints will have disappeared. It's going to snow again.'

'And then there was the dog,' Alice continued, pulling on her shoes. 'Ugh! They're wet.'

'But what's so special about a dog in the middle of the country? It could belong to anyone.'

'But it was . . . I don't know how to explain . . . it was like it knew me already.'

'Oh, honestly,' Mary said and, crossing to the wardrobe, she took out a red dress on a hanger and crossed to hang it from a beam in front of the window.

'What on earth are you doing?' William asked her, despairingly.

'It got creased in my case. I want to wear it at Christmas, if you must know,' Mary told him.

'But why are you hanging it there?'

'To air it.'

William and Alice exchanged a pitying look and William tapped his forehead.

'D'you think there's any hope for her, Will?' Alice asked in a hushed voice.

William shook his head, gravely.

'She'll definitely have to be put in the loony bin. Poor thing.'

'Poor thing,' Alice echoed and she sobbed dramatically.

'Oh, shut up, both of you.' Mary was losing her temper. 'If you think I'm loony, what about you two? Alice with disappearing footsteps and you, Will, with a disappearing man.'

'And the fox, Mary,' William shouted back, losing his temper.

'You saw a fox, so what's so special about that?'

'It looked at me. And the owl did. They looked at me, Mary,' then he lowered his voice to a hushed whisper, 'as if they were expecting me.'

'And my dog did,' Alice chimed in, not wanting to be left out of the story.

The three children looked at each other in silence for a moment.

'But, what could it mean?' Mary asked. 'Why do all the animals look at you and who was the man?'

'I don't know,' William said, quietly, 'but I'll tell you something. If he'd got on to the train at the station, I'd have heard the door slam. And I didn't, I know I didn't. And, if he disappeared there, then – why couldn't he do it again? Out there in the snow this morning.'

'Oh, Will,' Mary said in a whisper, 'it isn't going to be frightening, is it?'

'I don't think so,' her brother replied. 'They all seemed friendly . . .'

'Who all?' Mary cut in, nervously.

'The fox and the owl . . .'

'And my dog was very friendly,' Alice added, eagerly.

'And the man?' Mary asked, looking back at William.

'He was quite friendly,' William replied after a moment's thought. 'But he was a bit sort of . . . stern, as well. Like a . . . teacher . . . you know? He sort of stared at me . . .'

'But that's what you said the fox did.'

'It was the same. Exactly the same.'

They lapsed into silence again, all of them deep in thought and that was how Phoebe found them when she came into the room.

'Oh, what a fright you gave me,' she exclaimed. 'I thought you must have gone out. It was so quiet up here. Are you all right?'

'Yes thank you, Phoebe.' William answered for all of them.

'Jack's going into the town. You can go with him, if you like. I've made some hot chocolate. Come on down. It's much warmer in the kitchen.'

'Phoebe,' Alice asked her, as she was about to leave the room. 'Is there a big black and white dog that lives somewhere around here?'

'You've seen him?' Phoebe asked her, surprised. 'Jack

says I made him up. I've seen him often. I don't know where he comes from.'

'Maybe he lives here,' William said, on an impulse.

'Well, he'd be very welcome, but he won't ever come in. I've tried to persuade him. I worry about him, if he's a stray, particularly in this weather.'

'Would it be all right if I brought him in?' Alice asked her. 'He seems to like me.'

'You'll have to persuade Jack first. He says he doesn't want any animals in the house until he's finished doing all the repair work. And of course, with the baby coming . . . But I'd like an animal here. Particularly when Jack goes away.'

'D'you get scared here?' Alice asked her, her eyes wide.

Phoebe looked at her thoughtfully for a moment.

'I don't think the house has accepted us yet,' she replied in a grave tone. 'But I'm sure it will.' Then she smiled. 'I expect you'll all help. I think houses like young people. And this one has been empty for such a long time, and before that it was old people who lived here.'

'Did they die here?' Mary asked, fearfully.

'I expect so,' Phoebe replied, brightly. 'But there's nothing frightening about that. Death is a natural end to life, that's all. It isn't frightening. Come on. If we stand here talking, the hot chocolate will be cold chocolate!'

She went out of the room.

'I don't want to go into the town, William,' Mary whispered. 'I want to stay here and see the footprints.'

'You believe me,' Alice whispered gladly.

Mary nodded solemnly.

'What changed your mind?' Alice whispered.

Mary shrugged and frowned.

'The way Phoebe spoke. I think she knows something too.'

'What d'you mean, Mare?' William asked.

'I don't know. It's just a feeling.'

Jack set off for the town after they'd all had hot chocolate and biscuits together in the kitchen.

'As much as anything, I want to see the state of the road,' he explained.

'You're sure you don't need anything?' Phoebe asked the children. 'This will be the last chance before Christmas.'

But they had done their Christmas shopping. With their parents away in Africa, parcels had had to be sent well in advance and Mary had been commissioned to buy Jack and Phoebe a box of chocolates from them all. They'd all, of course, bought presents for each other.

'What size shoes do you all take?' Jack asked, as he was getting into the Land-Rover. 'I'd better get you some wellingtons. If this snow keeps up, you're going to need them.'

He drove slowly away from them down the drive,

the wheels cutting deep brown furrows in the snow.

'Come on,' William said, once the Land-Rover was out of sight, 'take us to see those tracks now, Alice. If we wait any longer the snow really will come down. We're going for a walk, Phoebe, is that all right?' he called through the kitchen door.

'Don't go too far, will you? The weather looks treacherous,' she called back. Then she added, 'Lunch is at one.'

'Lunch!' Alice protested under her breath. 'I expect it'll be cabbage AND carrots!' – two of her least favourite vegetables.

Then, leading the way, she ran across the snow-covered lawn, cutting off the circle of the drive, making for the footprints.

6

The Window

As Alice led the way up the steep hillside, following not only the mysterious footprints but also her own smaller ones, she pointed out the place where she had slipped and fallen and the scuffed snow where the dog had raced and jumped around her.

Then, reaching the clearing, she led them to the place where the prints dramatically ended.

'Now will you believe me?' she said, triumphantly.

'I didn't not believe you before, Al,' Mary protested. 'I just said that there was probably some simple explanation for it.'

'But what?' William said, staring at the snow, thoughtfully. Then he walked towards the trees on the other side of the clearing. Alice meanwhile crossed and placed her own feet in the final set of prints.

'Where are you?' she called in a loud voice.

'Don't, Alice,' William said, urgently.

'Why?' Alice asked, surprised.

'I don't like it. There's something . . . creepy about all this.'

'I'm not scared,' Alice said, sticking her hands into her anorak pockets.

'Hey, stay still a minute, Al,' Mary said suddenly and as she spoke, she ran towards her. 'D'you notice something different? About those footprints?'

Alice stared down at her own feet, standing in the printed snow.

'Um . . . whoever they belong to has got bigger feet than me.'

'Something else. Don't you see? All the way up from the drive the prints are one after another – because whoever made them was walking. But these last two are side by side.'

'So – the person was standing still,' William said, realizing what Mary was getting at.

'Exactly,' Mary said, excitedly. 'And something else. Look! Over there. What else can you see, Alice?'

Alice stared ahead of her, in the direction that Mary was pointing.

'I can see all sorts of things,' she replied. 'The trees, the snow . . .'

'What about the footprints?' She pointed to where the snow was all disturbed.

'No. They've disappeared. There's just a lot of mess, like as if the person had jumped from here to there and then fallen.'

William shook his head, and ran to where the snow

was all disturbed. Then he looked back at Alice, measuring the distance.

'No. It's too far. For someone to jump that far, they'd have to take a run first, and yet it's obvious they were standing still.'

'A human would have to take a run first,' Mary said quietly.

The other two looked at her.

'But whoever it is *must be* a human. Those are definitely human footsteps,' William protested.

'They are there, yes,' Mary agreed. 'But over here' – she ran to the disturbed snow – 'you can see animal prints. An animal could have jumped from where Alice is standing to here, couldn't it?'

'What sort of animal?' Alice asked in a scared voice.

'I don't know,' Mary shrugged, 'a big dog, maybe.'

'Mary,' Alice cried out, 'you mean the man turned into the dog?'

'I don't know,' Mary replied in a small voice. 'What d'you think, Will?'

'At the station, I was looking at the fox . . . and . . . it's so hard trying to remember exactly . . . I was staring at the fox, or rather the fox was staring at me . . . and . . . I heard the man's voice calling to me. I remember, for a moment, I thought the fox was speaking, then I realized that that wasn't possible. Then the fox disappeared, and I looked round and saw the man staring at me – just like the fox had been.'

William turned slowly and looked at Mary.

'So, the fox became the man? Is that what you think?' she asked him, quietly.

'I don't know what to think,' he answered her, thoughtfully.

'D'you mean the same man made these prints, then?' Alice asked. 'Or are there more than one . . . of them?'

'I don't know. I don't know,' William said, exasperatedly.

'You know what we're talking about, don't you?' Mary said, quietly.

'What, Mare?' Alice could hardly speak.

'Magic,' Mary answered.

Alice ran and grabbed hold of William's hand.

'Let's go back, William. I don't like it here.'

'Come on then,' her brother said and he sounded relieved at the suggestion.

They started off down the hill walking as quickly as they could. But they had to tread with care, for the snow was slippery and they didn't want to fall. Then Mary suddenly stopped.

'Oh, William,' she said, 'I've just thought of something else. The name of the station – Druce Coven.'

'What about it?' William asked her, his nervousness beginning to show in his voice.

'Don't you see? Coven. Witches have covens.'

With a shriek Alice set off at a run down the hill. She'd heard enough; she'd had enough and she didn't like any of it.

'Alice, wait for us,' William called. But she was already disappearing into the trees on the lower side of the clearing. Mary and he started off in pursuit, slipping and slithering down the slope into the darker wood.

Alice was waiting for them, panting and out of breath down on the drive. As William and Mary came out from the trees, the first light flakes of snow started to float down from above.

'I'm sorry,' Alice said, linking arms between them. 'I just didn't like it up there. I felt all the time we were being watched.'

'Come on, let's get back anyway. It'll be nearly lunch time.'

They walked in silence back along the drive towards the house. Then they paused for a moment, to look at it.

'It's ever such a big place just for Uncle Jack and Phoebe to live in,' Alice said.

'But they're going to make it into a hotel,' William said.

'Does that mean we'll have to pay every time we come to stay?' Mary asked.

'Of course not. We're family.'

'I don't think I'll like it when other people who we don't know are staying.'

'It won't be for ages yet,' William said, staring

thoughtfully at the place. 'Uncle Jack has masses of work to do on it, and he can't afford to employ a builder.'

'But he isn't a builder,' Mary said. 'I thought he was a scientist or something.'

'He makes bombs,' Alice said, sounding more cheerful.

'No, he doesn't, Alice. He was working with nuclear energy.'

'I thought that was bombs,' Alice said, kicking the snow.

'It's power and stuff. You know, like electricity.'

'Why has he stopped?' Mary asked. 'Mum said he was making a fortune.'

'He's dropped out,' William replied, without sounding absolutely certain himself what he meant. 'I think Phoebe maybe persuaded him.'

'But why?' Mary insisted.

William shrugged.

'Maybe she always wanted to run a hotel,' he said.

'I can't see it being much of a hotel,' Alice said, half to herself. 'Not if you can only eat vegetables all the time. Who would want that?'

'Other vegetarians,' William said, patiently.

'Are there any?' Alice asked, aghast.

'Masses,' William said. 'I expect some of your friends are.'

'They are not,' she retorted, witheringly. 'All my friends eat sausages. I make it a rule. Besides – what do vegetarians eat for Christmas dinner?'

'Stuffed cabbage, I expect,' William replied with a grin.

'Ugh!' Alice yelled, making instant sick noises.

Mary, who had been silent throughout this exchange, now gripped William's arm.

'William,' she said quietly, 'can you see something odd? About the house?'

'Oh, please! Not more frightenings,' Alice pleaded.

'What?' William asked, staring at it.

'Just look for a minute,' Mary told him. 'You too, Alice. I'm sure I'm right.'

The snow was falling thickly now. The house was grey against the whiteness. The centre of the building, where the porch was, was built of stone and looked almost like a church. It rose to the steeply pitched tiled roof in which their bedroom windows were set. To each side of this main section there were additional wings. One was built of wooden beams, painted black, with white plaster-work between them.

'That'll be the Tudor bit,' William said, knowledge-ably. 'Uncle Jack said that the centre bit is much older. Medieval, probably. It looks as if it might have been a monastery building. Then Uncle Jack said that the roof, where we are, was added to the main building at the same time as the Tudor bit . . .'

'Oh, we don't want a history lesson, Will,' Alice groaned.

'I think it's interesting. I could tell you weren't listening when he told us about it last night.'

'I was busy chewing the cud!' Alice giggled.

'Actually, the banana tart was delicious,' Mary said.

'Oooh, yes!' Alice agreed, rubbing her tummy.

'And then the other wing was added later,' William continued. 'But I can't remember when exactly. Anyway, what am I supposed to be noticing?'

'Shall I tell you?' Mary asked, smugly.

'Go on then,' William told her.

'Well. You see our windows.' She pointed up to the snowy roof where a row of dormer windows perched precariously on the steep slope. 'I know that one's ours, because I can see my red dress.'

'So?' William said, irritated by all this mystery.

'Well,' Mary continued, 'didn't you think we were right at the top of the house?'

'We are. We're right under the roof.'

'Well, I can see another window, higher up,' Mary said triumphantly.

'Where?' Alice demanded.

'You see the chimney?' Mary said, pointing again.

The other two peered through the thick blobs of snowflakes that were floating down in a steady stream. Above the dormer windows, a great stack of red brick chimneys rose from the centre of the roof. They were like a bundle of barley-sugar sticks, each one designed with a twisting shape and surmounted by chimney pots that looked like spiky crowns.

'Yes,' William said, focusing on the chimneys.

'Well, can't you see? At the base of the chimneys. Where the red brick meets the line of the roof . . .'

'I can see it now, Mare. Yes, you're right. There's a little window set into the base of the chimney. Or, at least, it looks like a window.'

'I'm sure it is,' Mary said. 'But, how can there be a room there? And, how d'you get to it?'

'There must be a way up to it from our landing. We'll explore later,' William said.

'There must be ever such a lot of secret rooms,' Alice said, brushing soft snow off her sleeve. 'I expect you could almost get lost just being in the house.'

'Right. Let's make a vow, then,' William said, using his stern voice.

'Solemn honour?' Alice asked, catching his tone.

'Solemn honour,' William repeated.

The three stretched out their right hands and then clasped them together; Mary's on William's and Alice's on Mary's.

'We solemnly swear,' William intoned and the girls repeated after him, 'that no one will explore the house or the country round it on their own . . .'

'What? Not ever?' Alice exclaimed.

'Not ever,' William insisted.

'Oh, William!'

'Swear, Alice.'

'But it's so boring having to do everything all together. We'd never have seen the footprints if I hadn't come out on my own . . .'

'Swear, Alice,' he repeated.

'D'you think it's really dangerous?' Mary asked him.

'I don't know. But, like we said, there's something very odd about this place. It may not be bad but until we know I think we should be careful.'

'All right,' Alice said, her eyes wide with fear, 'I'm ready to swear now.'

'We solemnly swear,' they said in unison.

As the children hurried round to the kitchen door, the fox which had been watching from the shelter of a holly bush turned and streaked away up the snow-covered slope into the secret depths of the forest.

'What was that?' Mary said, looking over her shoulder.

'What was what?' Alice asked. She sounded as though she'd had enough excitement for one day.

'Oh, nothing. It's all right,' Mary said, quietly. 'I thought I saw something, that's all.'

'Oh, come on, then,' Alice pleaded. 'I'm freezing,' and she ran ahead towards the house.

'What was it?' William enquired under his breath.

'Fox, I think,' Mary said, trying to sound nonchalant.

William nodded.

'I knew he was there,' he said. 'I just knew it.'

'Let's go in, Will,' Mary whispered. 'Alice is right. It is cold.'

But William knew that it wasn't just the cold that made her hurry forward.

'What does it want?' he said, half to himself.

'Us, I think,' his sister answered and she ran towards the kitchen door.

7

The Attic Rooms

Jack didn't return in time for lunch. Phoebe waited as long as she could, then she told the children that they should all eat and that she'd heat something for him when he arrived.

'I expect the road is bad over the moor, with all this snow,' she said. 'He's been worried about what it would be like ever since we moved in. On account of the baby, I suppose. But, honestly! People were having babies long before there were hospitals and cars to get them there. Poor Jack! I can see him being the midwife himself before we're through!'

'But it's not for ages,' Mary said. 'I expect the snow will have gone by then.'

'End of January?' Phoebe said, with a smile. 'Could be worse than this.'

'Poor Uncle Jack,' Alice murmured.

'Why, Alice?' Phoebe asked, looking at her.

'He's not a doctor, is he?' Alice tried not to let the animosity she was feeling sound in her voice. 'I'm not surprised he's worried.'

'I'll be all right,' Phoebe told her.

'Maybe he's not just thinking of you,' Alice retorted. 'It's his baby as well, you know.'

This unexpected outburst was followed by an awkward silence. Alice chopped up her food energetically, then pushed it to the side of her plate.

'Don't you like it?' Phoebe said, after a moment.

'I'm not hungry,' Alice replied.

'I think it's delicious,' Mary said. 'What is it, Phoebe?'

'Oh, just lentils and vegetables and things.'

'Honestly,' Mary continued, warming dangerously to the subject, 'you wouldn't know it didn't have meat in it.'

'I would,' Phoebe said, with a smile.

'So would I,' Alice agreed.

'Is eating meat so important to you, Alice?' Phoebe asked, turning to look at her, still smiling.

Alice shrugged and looked down at her plate, her lips pursed.

A horrible, embarrassed silence followed. William glanced at Mary, as if willing her to say something. But she just looked at her fingernails and pretended she hadn't seen him.

'I don't eat meat because I would find it impossible to kill the animal I was eating. That being so, it doesn't seem right to me that I should ask someone else to do the killing for me. I also believe that you can get as good, if not better nutrition, from a meat-free diet. Doesn't that seem reasonable to you?'

The question was directed at Alice, who said nothing and remained staring at her plate. After another interminable silence, Phoebe rose and went to the stove for the casserole dish.

'Would either of you like a second helping?' she said, addressing William and Mary.

'No thank you,' William said, trying to sound cheerful. 'I'm full up.'

'Mary?' Phoebe held the casserole dish towards her. Mary shook her head, still staring at her nails. Phoebe sighed.

'I haven't made a pudding,' she said. 'We have our main meal in the evening. But there are some apples . . .'

'Is it all right if we get down now?' William asked.

'Of course.'

'We'll do the washing-up,' Mary volunteered half-heartedly.

'No, you won't,' Phoebe said, firmly. 'You're on holiday.' She glanced out of the low window at the frosty yard and the falling snow. 'Though I don't know what you're going to do with yourselves. I'd hoped you could go for long walks and other equally healthy things! But I expect you'd find that boring. Though, actually, the country round here is really exciting. But in this weather that won't be much fun. In fact I'm not at all sure it wouldn't be dangerous.' She rose and walked over to lean against the sink, looking out at the wintry scene. 'I hope Jack *is* all right,' she said, more to herself.

Behind her back Alice looked up for the first time and pulled a hideous face and stuck her tongue out. Mary, seeing this, almost giggled and put a hand over her mouth.

'Can we go upstairs and play?' William asked, innocently.

'Play?' Mary exploded, scornfully. 'I don't play, William!'

'Yes, you do,' her brother said, giving her a savage look. 'I brought Trivial Pursuits.'

'It's too difficult, William,' she wailed. 'And you've learned all the answers.'

'Come on,' he said, with a meaningful look. 'Is it all right, Phoebe?'

'But won't you be cold?' she asked, turning to look at them. 'We aren't really prepared yet for cold weather. Jack is going to light a log fire in the hall for Christmas. But really, this is the only warm place. Would you like to play in here?'

'No, it's all right, thank you,' he said, leading the way towards the door.

Mary followed then Alice slid off her chair and ran after them.

'Alice,' Phoebe called to her. 'Please let's be friends.'

But Alice pushed past William and out through the door into the hall. Phoebe looked disappointed and crossed to start clearing the table.

'Light the electric fire up there, won't you?' she said to William, as he followed his sisters out of the kitchen, closing the door after him.

'I hate her. I hate her. I hate her,' Alice sobbed, lying face down on her bed and kicking her feet.

William and Mary sat on Mary's bed, watching her, glumly.

'I hate her and I hate it here and I wish Mum and Dad hadn't gone to Africa and . . . oh . . .' A great wave of sobbing choked her words.

Still William and Mary remained silent. William had stuck his hands into his trouser pockets and Mary was sitting on hers.

'Uncle Jack must be mad,' Alice started again. 'He must be mad. Of all the horrible women to pick to live with . . . No wonder he hasn't married her. I don't blame him one little bit. If it wasn't for the baby on the way . . . I bet it's a horrible baby, with a mother like that. Oh, William . . .' and as she said his name, Alice sat bolt upright, wide-eyed and shattered by a thought that had suddenly occurred to her. 'William,' she said again, this time in a frightened whisper, 'd'you suppose she's a witch? I bet she is. I bet that's what it's all about. Phoebe's a witch. She's probably put Uncle Jack under some awful spell and forced him to give her a baby and to come and live with her in this horrible house and eat nothing but cabbage and carrots for the rest of his life.' Alice sniffed and wiped her tear-stained face with the back of her hands.

The other two continued to stare at her as before. Long practice had taught them that the best way to deal with Alice's tantrums was to wait for them to go away. If you said anything, anything at all, it only added fuel to the fire. The best thing to do was wait.

'Well, I think she is,' Alice spat at them, disconcerted by their silence. She sniffed and wiped her nose with a hanky. 'I shall starve to death as well. Then you'll be sorry. I'll just disappear from lack of food.'

'Ally, you don't even like meat much,' William said, testing the water.

'I love meat,' Alice rounded on him with renewed vigour. 'Everyone knows how much I adore sausages. They're my favourite, favourite food. That year we had sausages and potatoes cooked in the bonfire was the best meal I've ever had. Oh, I wish Mum and Dad were here,' and then she added in a desperately sad voice, 'It's going to be a horrible Christmas.' She started to cry again, but this time, more quietly; this time real tears.

William crossed over to her bed and sat beside her, putting an arm round her.

'Don't cry,' he said gently, 'please don't cry, Ally. You

promised Mum and Dad that you wouldn't. They had to go – because they're needed over there. Thousands of people are dying in Africa from the famine and because there aren't enough doctors or medicine. Mum and Dad had to go because, maybe, they'll be able to help a bit. Oh, Alice, please don't cry,' and as he spoke he could feel a tight lump in the back of his throat and he had to swallow hard to stop tears coming into his own eyes.

'Come on,' Mary said, standing up. 'Let's try to find that room.'

'What room?' Alice asked, blowing her nose again.

'The one that's up above us,' Mary replied thoughtfully. As she spoke she stared up at the roof.

'I never really saw the window,' Alice said, still sounding miserable. 'You're sure it is there?'

'A little round window, right at the bottom of the chimneys,' Mary insisted, 'where the roof meets the bricks. It looked almost like part of the pattern of the brick base. It is there. Isn't it, Will?'

'Maybe there was a room up in the eaves and at some time it was removed,' William suggested.

'But, how d'you know it isn't still there?' Alice asked, now also staring at the roof above them.

'That's easy. You can see that, in here, the roof goes up to a point, can't you? There's no space for another room.'

'Where do the chimneys come up?' Mary said, crossing to the door and going out on to the landing. The other two followed her.

It was dark on the landing. William flicked the light switch. Nothing happened.

'Bulb must have gone,' he said. 'Leave the door open, Alice,' and as he spoke he opened his bedroom door also and that of the bathroom, which had a window looking out over the back of the house. The light filtering from the three rooms filled the landing with half shadows.

'That's odd,' William said. 'There are two rooms at the front, right? Yours and mine. But there's only one room, the bathroom, at the back. Oh, of course. My room isn't as big as yours. And' – as he spoke he went into the bathroom – 'the rest of the space in here is taken up by that brick wall. That's it,' he said with a gesture. 'The chimneys.'

'Where?' Alice asked. Staring at the wall.

'Behind this wall. And' – he hurried into his room – 'here is another side of the same brick square.' Then he went and opened his bedroom window and leaned out. A cold gust of wind blew in and a powdering of snow fell on to the sill.

'Be careful, Will. It's ever so steep,' Mary said, pulling her cardigan round her against the cold.

'What are you looking for?' Alice asked, trying to squeeze out of the small opening beside him.

'Just a minute, Al,' he said. 'Yes, I thought so. The roof goes much further along.' William came back into the room and crossed to the side wall, opposite the door. He tapped the wall. 'It doesn't sound hollow,' he said thoughtfully.

'But why should it? Oh, one of you explain, please,' Alice pleaded.

'I could show you from outside,' William said.

'I'm not going out there, it's freezing. And close the window, William,' Mary said, shivering and running back to the warmth of the electric fire in the girls' room. William and Alice followed after her.

'Go on, tell us, Will, please,' Alice said again.

'Well,' William began, 'you remember how the centre of the house is like a stone tower? Like a monastery tower only not very high?' The girls nodded. 'Well, that's taken up by the big hall downstairs, with that sort of gallery round it that's now used as a landing. I think that must be the only bit of the medieval building that's left. Then the bedrooms below here are in the Tudor wing.'

'That's where Uncle Jack sleeps,' Mary said, working it out as he spoke.

'Right,' William agreed.

'With her,' Alice said and made an elaborate sick sound.

'Don't start that again, Alice, please,' William begged,

trying not to lose his train of thought. 'The rooms on the other side of the hallway, round the gallery, are in the opposite wing. I think Uncle Jack said it was added in George the First's reign. But we don't need to bother about those. When the Tudor bit was added, they decided to make the house higher than the stone tower. So they put these attic rooms on, stretching over the Tudor bit and also over the top of the tower. Our bedrooms are really over the Tudor bit. Right? Except a bit of the bathroom and a bit of my bedroom. OK? But if you look out of my window, the roof stretches on beyond the side wall of the bathroom and my room, to the other side of the main tower. So there has to be more space there. You see? A bit that isn't accounted for. In other words,' William concluded triumphantly, 'more rooms.'

The girls blinked at him with looks of utter confusion.

'I don't see . . . I mean there are probably more rooms the other side of this wall as well,' Mary said, tapping the side wall of the room they were in.

'Of course there are. You can see the windows along the roof,' William agreed.

'So?' Mary asked.

'There's probably a staircase further along in the Tudor wing that will lead up to them. But – where's the staircase to the bit on the other side of my room? There can't be one. The only stairs up to here are the ones we use.'

'I know. I know,' Alice cried. 'Maybe there was a

door once up here that went through and someone blocked it up.'

'Yes,' William agreed, 'but what a funny thing to do. To seal off rooms so that no one can get into them. I mean, what's in there? Why did they seal them off? Maybe they were trying to hide something? But, if so – what?'

They looked at one another in silence.

'Oh, Will,' Mary said at last. 'I'm glad it's your side of the landing,' and Alice moved closer to her sister and took hold of her hand.

'This is a really creepy place,' she said in a small voice. 'I think I'm a bit scared.'

'It's all right, Al,' William said, sounding far from certain about the statement. 'There's bound to be some simple explanation.' Then he got up and ran to the window. 'Uncle Jack's back,' he said with relief as he saw the Land-Rover skid to a halt on the drive.

8

Uncle Jack's Discoveries

The road over the moor had not been too bad on Jack's outward journey. There had been a certain amount of drifting snow during the night, but the Land-Rover managed to cling to the icy surface and he had got to the town in good time.

'But what I hadn't reckoned,' he told them, 'is how much the weather can vary in the mountains. There was bright sunshine down there. It never entered my head that it would be snowing up on the tops!'

Consequently, he'd been in no hurry to get back. When he'd completed the shopping, which included three pairs of wellingtons for the children, he'd called in at the Local History Museum. The librarian there, a woman called Miss Prewett, had promised to get him a copy of a book that referred to Golden House and the valley and would give him, she thought, quite a lot of interesting bits of history about the house.

Miss Prewett turned out to be highly delighted when he arrived.

'It's all so exciting,' she exclaimed as soon as she had

made him a cup of coffee and he was sitting in her office facing her across the desk. 'I managed to get hold of that book I mentioned. It belongs to Major Blenkins, but he's so old now he'd forgotten that he'd even got it. His housekeeper found it for me. Of course we must return it eventually, but he's happy for you to borrow it for as long as you like to.' She slammed her hands down on top of her desk and raised her eyes to the ceiling. 'But, my dear Mr' – she fumbled in her own mind, trying to remember Jack's surname, which she was unable to recall, if indeed she had ever known it – 'of course, I've only glanced at this' – she indicated a thick, battered book that was lying on the desk in front of her – 'and I warn you, it's a bit of a plod, written at the turn of the century by a Jonas Lewis, who had probably quite a bright mind but was not what you might call a natural writer . . . Oh, it's fascinating.' She pulled the book towards her and started flicking through the pages. 'Privately produced, of course. I believe the Major bought it at an auction, years ago.' She shook her head and sighed, as she moved the pages. 'So much I didn't know. Well, to tell you the truth, I didn't know any of it. You see the title?' She held up the book so that Jack got a quick glimpse of the faded cover and then put it back on the desk before he had a chance to read anything that might have been written on it. 'Well, there you are. What a bit of luck, don't you agree?'

Jack tried several times during the early stages of the interview to interrupt her, but he soon realized that it was useless.

'Do you know anything about the subject?' she asked him suddenly, blinking as she looked at him through her small wire spectacles.

Jack was so surprised to be directly addressed that it took him a moment to respond. When he did, he realized that he hadn't a clue what she was talking about.

'I'm terribly sorry, Miss Prewett. What subject?' he said, a little breathlessly.

'This, nincom!' she cried, slapping the book in front of her and smiling at him at the same time. 'Alchemy, man. Haven't you listened to a word I've been saying?'

'Alchemy?' Jack had responded, totally at sea now. 'The book is about alchemy?'

'No, no, no, no,' Miss Prewett cried. Then, 'Well, yes, in a way it is. But think, man. What do you know about alchemy?'

'Well, not a lot, actually,' Jack replied, trying desperately to remember anything at all about the subject. 'Wasn't it the . . . the forerunner of chemistry . . . ?'

'Go on,' Miss Prewett said, nodding her head vigorously.

'The alchemists believed that they had discovered a way of turning base metals into gold. That's all I know.'

'Quite, I expect that's all any of us know, really. All

a lot of nonsense, I dare say, and frankly I think a rather dubious occupation. All that glisters is not gold, you know. If, of course, that is all there was to it.' She paused for a moment, considering, then shook her head, seeming mentally to change the subject. 'But think, Mr . . .' She stopped again and looked at him. 'I'm so sorry . . . what is your name?'

'Green,' Jack replied. 'Jack Green.'

'Is it? I never knew that. I'm not sure I can even guarantee I'll remember it in the future. Think, Mr . . .' She waved her hand; she'd forgotten it already. 'The name of your house, man?'

'Golden House in Golden Valley,' and as Jack spoke what she was trying to tell him fell into place.

'This book is called *The Alchemical Writings of Jonas Lewis*. See here, the title page,' and opening the book, she pushed it across to Jack's side of the desk. Jack stood up and turned the book in order that he could read:

'The Alchemical Writings of Jonas Lewis, of The House in Golden Valley. Being completed this last day of the last year of the century, 31st December, 1899.'

'Isn't it thrilling?' Miss Prewett said, looking at him again. 'Of course, he was probably a maniac, but – a book written in and about your house; well, not about it, exactly, but it does explain the name. Of course, this little chappy – Jonas thing – may just have been making capital out of the place. After all, there are records of a house called Gelden Place on the site as far back as 1350.'

'Where would this reference be, please?' Jack asked.

'In the parish records. I made some notes for you,' Miss Prewett said, sliding an envelope towards him across the surface of the desk. 'All the owners of Gelden Place, later called Golden House, are listed there for you. The house name was changed during the reign of Henry the Eighth; before that it was some sort of religious establishment, I think. Not a monastery, exactly, but a place of retreat. I suppose it fell into disuse at the dissolution. How is your history, Mr . . . ? You remember the dates? The Dissolution of the Monasteries? 1536 to 1540? You'll have to do some mugging up, I'm afraid. I'm a bit rusty, so no good relying on me. The most people want to know now is what time the tea shop opens at Hope Castle and whether the piece of stone they've dug up in their garden might perhaps be a prehistoric spearhead. It never is, of course, but they don't want to believe me. However, what little I could glean is written down in there. If you can read my writing. I have to admit I have a job sometimes myself. It's the sign of a quick mind, they say. But I rather think it's an indication of supreme sloppiness. To think that I had the makings of a scholar. Too bad. The waste, the waste. Never mind. Over to you, then. Good hunting!'

'You've been most kind,' Jack said, rising and taking the envelope and slipping it between the pages of the book. 'I'll take great care of the book and return it soon in the new year.'

'I shouldn't worry too much. I can't help feeling the book belongs in your house anyway. You'll see what I mean when you read it. Terribly heavy going' – she lowered her voice again – 'I actually very much like the writings of Agatha Christie. Do you read her? Frightfully good. I like a good murder, personally. But of course, here, I let it appear that I'm steeped in historical research. I used to be, Mr Lewis' – she beamed at Jack, having obviously decided that any surname was better than none – 'but that was when I was a girl. With age I have realized that a good murder mystery is far more satisfying. You see, if you can't work it out for yourself, you're usually given the answer – whodunnit, you know – by the end of the book. With history, we will never know whodunnit. In the end, I find that rather frustrating.'

She was still talking when Jack left the office. He wondered if she'd noticed that he'd gone.

He'd spent far longer with her than he'd meant to and when he turned the Land-Rover off the forest road and started to climb up towards the moor, he was horrified to discover that near blizzard conditions were raging, through which he'd only just managed to drive.

'Are we going to be snowed in?' Phoebe asked, quietly.

'We will be by the morning, I'm afraid,' Jack replied grimly.

They both glanced at the children, who were seated round the table in the kitchen, listening to his story.

'But not to worry,' Jack told them, lightly. 'We've plenty of food and I'm going to light a fire in the hall. That should warm the whole house. And we can sit in front of it and . . . play games, or whatever.' He smiled at them and shrugged.

'Have you got television?' Mary asked, cheerfully.

Jack pulled a glum face and shook his head.

'Doesn't matter,' Mary said, trying to make it sound as if she meant it.

'I tell you what,' Jack said, 'after supper, we could have a look at the book.'

'Oooh, yes!' the three children chorused, sounding surprisingly keen.

'They won't want some stuffy old book,' Phoebe said.

'Yes we will,' William protested. 'We want to know everything there is to know about this place,' and, as he spoke, he looked at his sisters, implying that they should say no more.

'Aren't we going to tell Uncle Jack about the missing room?' Mary asked him, later, when they were upstairs in their room waiting to be called to supper.

'Let's not say anything yet,' he replied. 'Let's find out as much as we can first. You know what grown-ups are like. They'll only want to take over and make out they knew all about it already.'

Alice suddenly sighed loudly and then groaned.

'Did you see what Phoebe was washing at the sink? Parsnips! That's all there'll be for supper! Parsnips! Big deal! You're not to sit near me, William. Parsnips make you poop all the time!' And she shook with laughter.

9

Jonas Lewis's Book

As soon as supper was finished, the children helped Phoebe to clear the table. It had been decided that they would spend the evening in the kitchen and not light the fire until the following day.

'But if you light a fire in the hall tomorrow night,' Phoebe protested, 'how will Father Christmas get down the chimney? It's Christmas Eve tomorrow.'

Alice winced and looked away. She was sure that this statement was intended for her. It embarrassed her that Phoebe should so obviously think of her as a child, but at the same time she didn't want to get into another argument with her and so she tried to remain silent.

'Don't be silly,' Jack said. 'He waits until it's gone out. That's why he comes in the middle of the night.'

'It'll be awfully sooty. I'd better put some old sheets down. Don't you agree, Alice?'

Alice scratched her cheek and looked at the floor.

'Never mind the sheets, don't forget a tot of brandy and a mince pie,' Jack said, continuing the absurd game.

'There is no Father Christmas,' Alice said at last, unable to contain herself any longer.

'Alice!' Phoebe cried. 'What are you saying? No Father Christmas?'

'Of course there isn't. It's just a story for little children. And I am not one. Honestly, Phoebe. I am eight, you know.'

Phoebe looked exasperated and was about to snap some remark at Alice, but Jack cut in, changing the subject.

'Well, anyway, I won't light a fire in the hall tonight. I'll need help getting logs in and it's snowing heavens high out there. So, if you don't all mind sitting in the kitchen . . .'

And so the table was cleared and a piece of clean cloth was spread so that Jonas Lewis's book wouldn't get dirty and the children sat close to Jack as he pulled the lamp over and opened the covers.

'*The Alchemical Writings of Jonas Lewis,*' Uncle Jack read, in a quiet voice.

'What does alchemical mean?' William asked.

'To do with alchemy,' his uncle replied. 'Alchemy was supposed to be the ancient art of changing worthless metals into gold.'

'What? You mean any metal? Like a tin or something?' William asked.

'I suppose so,' Jack answered.

'But then you'd be richer than anyone else in the

world,' Mary cried. 'Is it make-believe?'

'Sounds like it to me,' Jack said, flicking through the thick pages.

Some of them were covered with drawings, so faded that it was difficult to make out exactly what they were meant to represent.

'That's a dragon,' Alice squealed at one.

Much of the text was in a foreign language.

'*Finis corruptionis et principio generationis*,' Jack read from one page with difficulty. 'Anyone any good at Latin?'

The children shook their heads.

Phoebe was sitting at the other end of the kitchen table, sewing the hems of the curtains for the kitchen window. She wasn't interested in the book, she'd said, but now she looked up.

'Say it again, Jack.'

'*Finis corruptionis* . . .' Jack began. But Phoebe rose and came and stood behind him, looking over his shoulder. The book was open at a drawing in a circle. The circle had signs all round it.

'The signs of the zodiac,' Phoebe said. 'What we call the birth signs. And in the middle the sun and the moon, locked in struggle with the dragon forces. The dragons represent nature, and the sun and the moon are sulphur and quicksilver.'

Jack looked at her in amazement.

'How do you know all that?' he asked.

Phoebe shrugged and frowned slightly.

'I don't remember,' she answered him. 'It's almost as though I've seen it before. But if I have, I can't remember where. Anyway, I'm probably wrong. It's just a way of interpreting the picture. But probably not the only way. As for the words, let me see.' She smiled at Jack. 'I was good at Latin once.' She looked at the page again. 'The end of corruption and the beginning of generation,' she translated. Then she frowned. 'Well, that's what it says. But, what does it mean, I wonder?'

'What does any of it mean?' Jack asked, flicking on through the pages. 'These look like a lot of sums. And this, some kind of chemical formula.'

'Well, you're a chemist, Jack,' Phoebe said, returning to her sewing. 'Can't you make sense of it?'

'I haven't a clue what it means,' Jack murmured, reading as he spoke. 'This seems to be instructions about the amount of heat required . . . The letters are so faded.' He angled the page towards the lamp. 'Yes, you were right, Phoebe. That word is quicksilver. How on earth did you know?'

'I'm sure I've seen a drawing like it somewhere before.' Phoebe frowned as she spoke, trying to remember. 'What is quicksilver?'

'Mercury,' Jack answered her.

'The stuff you have in thermometers?' William asked.

'That's it,' Jack said, flicking on through the book.

'It's ever such a boring book, isn't it?' Mary said, yawning.

'You tired, Mary?' Phoebe asked her.

'A bit,' Mary answered.

'This part is like a diary,' Jack said, continuing to look at the book. '"October 9th, 1899. Monday. It has worked. Our problems are at an end. Crawden will be paid. Praise be to God!" . . . Crawden? That's the name of the old lady who used to live here.'

Jack flicked on, then stopped, reading again:

'"October 20th. A dull day. Crawden comes tomorrow. The dog was up on the ridge. I took out my shooter, but missed him again. God curse him. I must do what I must do. If Crawden is not paid, then everything will go."'

'What's it about, Uncle Jack?' Alice asked, sounding scared.

'Who's Crawden?' William asked.

'He must be a relative of the previous owner of the house. All we know is that Golden House was last occupied years ago, by an old lady called Miss Crawden,' Jack explained.

'But that was ages ago, Jack,' Phoebe cut in, carrying on with her sewing.

'The dog, Will. It mentioned the dog,' Alice whispered.

Phoebe looked up, surprised.

'The dog?' she said. 'No. He mustn't shoot the dog,' and then she looked down again, wishing she hadn't spoken. Alice watched her through half-closed eyes, her head resting on her arm as if she was falling asleep.

Jack turned more pages until he was nearly at the end of the book.

'"All is lost,"' he read. '"The gold has reverted. Crawden has come to me. I think he knows what has taken place. He will take the house in payment. All is lost. I am finished. Fool's gold. Fool's gold."'

Then he turned to the last page of all.

'"Whoever reads this let him take heed. The Gold is not for use. The Magus watches. The Magus knows. The Magus owns us all. I am ruined. May the Lord God have mercy upon my soul."'

Jack closed the book and for a moment there was silence in the kitchen.

'What's a Magus, Uncle Jack?' William asked.

'I'm not sure. A master, isn't it?' Jack directed his question at Phoebe, who had stopped sewing and was sitting, with her eyes lowered, seemingly lost in thought.

'Magus?' she said, after a moment. 'It's a wise man. Like the Magi in the Christmas story. A Magus is a magician.'

As she spoke Jack picked up the book and rose from the table. As he did so, a thick white envelope fell to the floor.

'I'd better put this somewhere safe,' he said, crossing

to the hall door. 'We'll look at it again in more detail another day.'

'You've dropped something, Uncle Jack,' Mary called, picking up the envelope.

'Did I? Oh, yes. Miss Prewett's homework. You can open it, if you like. It's a list of the names of all the people who have lived in the house over the years. I'm going to put this in the bookcase in the hall. Won't be a minute.'

'You, William. You open it,' Mary said, pushing the envelope towards him across the table.

'I think you should all go to bed. You've had quite enough excitement for one day,' Phoebe said, reaching across and taking the envelope. 'Plenty of time for this tomorrow,' and she placed it beside her sewing basket. 'Look at Alice, she's half asleep sitting there.'

'Oh, Phoebe,' William protested.

Just then the kitchen clock chimed ten.

'Time for bed,' Phoebe said. 'It's Christmas Eve tomorrow. Say good night to Jack.'

'Going to bed?' he asked, coming back into the room.

'Yes, Jack. It's time, I think.'

'Oh, please, Uncle Jack,' William pleaded. 'Let's just look at the list of names at least.'

But Phoebe looked up at Jack and shook her head.

'I can't disobey her,' Jack laughed. 'Phoebe's word is law around here! Besides, it is late. I feel ready for bed as well. Off you go. Good night, all of you.'

The children trooped out of the room, Mary supporting Alice, who was indeed half asleep as Phoebe had remarked. As they slowly climbed the stairs to the gallery they heard Jack say to Phoebe:

'What's the matter, darling?'

'Oh, Jack,' she answered him. 'You should never have brought that book here.'

'Why, what's the matter?'

William was standing on the gallery, listening now with Mary supporting Alice beside him.

'I'm frightened, Jack,' they heard Phoebe reply. 'That book, I don't know what it is about it – but it terrifies me. I wish you hadn't brought it, that's all . . .'

Then Phoebe appeared at the kitchen door, looking up at them. 'Go to bed, children. I told you. Go to bed.'

'Good night, Phoebe,' William called and he watched her as she went back into the kitchen, closing the door behind her. At once her voice was heard again. But now, with the door closed, it was impossible to make out the words being said.

'What was all that about?' Mary asked him.

'She knows something,' Alice said, surprising them with the sound of her voice.

'I thought you were asleep, Al,' William said.

'I was listening, that's all,' Alice replied. Then she continued in a low voice, 'She's a witch, William. I'm sure of it. She knew too much.'

'Come up to bed,' Mary said, fearfully.

'I wish we could get away from here,' Alice said.

'Well we can't,' William told her. 'And anyway, if she is a witch, I'm not leaving Uncle Jack on his own with her.'

'Come to bed, William,' Mary pleaded and she pushed him ahead of them up the narrow spiral staircase.

10

When William Can't Sleep

The snow made everything very quiet. The wind had stopped blowing and although the sky was heavy and overcast with clouds there was a strange luminous glow that filled the room with ghostly half light.

William switched on his torch and looked at his watch. It was two o'clock. The last time he had looked it had been one-thirty. He punched his pillow into a different shape and closed his eyes, willing himself to sleep. He tried to empty his mind. He tried to concentrate on his toes. He even tried counting sheep. But all was to no avail. Then he sat up. If he couldn't sleep, he decided he might just as well face up to the fact and not waste time trying. Pulling on his dressing gown, he felt under the bed for his slippers.

It was freezing in the room. He crossed over to the window without putting on the lamp and looked out. The snow that had fallen during the evening was piled up against the pane, obscuring most of the view. Through a small portion of an upper corner he could just see the snowy exterior and the dark clouds, scudding across a more distant sky.

It's like being wrapped in cotton wool, he thought.

He sat on the window sill and, switching on his torch again, he pointed at the side wall of the room. He hoped, perhaps, that he might see the outline of some blocked-off door. But the wall offered no hint of a way through to the rooms that he was certain lay beyond it. Then he pointed the thin, bright ray at the brick chimney breast that took up part of the back wall, behind his bed. The brick had been painted the same white as the rest of the walls but was still quite obviously brick, whereas the other walls were made of rough plaster. The steeply raked ceiling met the chimney in a rather uneven line. Somewhere, just above this point, he reckoned the little window was placed.

But what for? he thought. Why is there a window up there? A window in a chimney doesn't make sense. Unless . . .

He crossed and tapped at the bricks, listening but not quite sure what he was hoping to hear. Then he shook his head. It was hopeless. He opened the door and went out on to the landing.

William inched open the girls' door and looked in. The sound of regular breathing told him that both his sisters were fast asleep. This made him feel lonely. He half thought of waking them, but he knew that wouldn't be fair. He closed the door quietly again and stood for a moment on the landing.

His heart was beating loudly. He switched on the torch again. The walls of the spiral staircase sprang into relief in the light. They were made of grey stone and must have belonged to the original stone tower. As William looked at the walls he realized that the spiral had probably once been a turret onto the flat roof of the tower. He looked at the floor of the landing and noticed that the floor there was also stone-flagged. So, where he was standing had once been the open roof of the tower. He shivered and thought that it was almost as cold now as it would be being outside. Perhaps he should go back to bed and read. At least that would be warmer than wandering about in the middle of the night.

If they're going to turn this place into an hotel, he thought, they'll have to put in central heating.

Then, far below in the house, he heard the kitchen clock chime the half hour. Half past two. This is stupid, he thought, I'm definitely going back to bed. But instead he started to tiptoe down the stone stairs to the gallery below.

The great hall of the house was in darkness. William stood on the gallery landing and pointed his torch over and down into the space below. He moved the beam slowly round the room until it came to rest on the centre of the huge brick fireplace. The canopy over the opening

was decorated with carved brick work. There were dragons curling and catching at their tails and two snakes
climbing up a stick that stood above the dragons and
seemed to have been planted between them. On one side
of the snake stick a fat sun was carved with rays that
stretched out over the brick wall. On the other side of
the snake stick, a crescent moon was carved.

William was surprised to see this brick picture. He
was sure he should have noticed it before but couldn't
understand why he hadn't. Unless, he thought, it's something to do with the way the beam of light is falling on
it. Perhaps it's only visible in torch light and from up
here. I must remember to look in the morning.

He walked carefully along the gallery to the head of
the broad stairs that led down to the ground floor. At
first the silence of the sleeping house was overwhelm-
ing. But, as he listened, innumerable small sounds came
into his hearing. The clock ticking in the kitchen. A
floorboard creaking along the gallery. The faint, hollow
moaning of the night air in the chimney. Even the regular, heavy breathing from Jack and Phoebe's room.

William slowly descended the stairs. The hall, like
most of the house, was only sparsely furnished. There
was a long oak table running along the centre of the
hall, with tall-backed chairs arranged round it. Two old
armchairs, with wooden arms and padded backs and
seats, stood either side of the hearth and between them,

in front of the fireplace, there was a long, low oak stool covered in a similar needlework to the armchairs. On either side of the front door, narrow arched windows gave a small amount of light during daytime. But the hall would always be a gloomy place. The floor, which was stone-flagged, was inadequately covered with a few thin rugs which did nothing to stop the extreme cold that seeped up out of the ground below. The wall opposite the fireplace was taken up for the most part by a huge bookcase which stretched from the floor up to the height of the kitchen door. Another door, leading, William guessed, to the rooms at the front of the Tudor wing of the house, was situated at the other end of this bookcase. The shelves were already well stacked with books, but William had little difficulty in locating the one for which he was looking.

Jack had placed Jonas Lewis's book on its side on the lowest shelf. It was still wrapped in the piece of material that Phoebe had placed on the kitchen table to prevent it getting dirty. William was surprised to discover how heavy the book was. He had to use both his hands to lift it. He had intended to take it back up to his room, but instead he placed it on the oak table and, holding the torch in one hand, he slowly turned the pages with the other.

As he did so, he discovered the envelope, which Phoebe had stopped them opening, lodged between the pages. It had been torn open, presumably by her or Jack after the children had gone to bed. William laid the envelope to one side and continued to look through the book.

The text was all written in small, cramped letters and he soon wearied of trying to decipher it. He had meant to start reading from the beginning but quickly started skipping from page to page, looking only at the diagrams and drawings.

There were numerical tables and geometric charts. There were drawings of flowers and animals. And then moving further into the book he came upon a whole page devoted to a rough sketch that had obviously been altered many times. Two dragons writhed at the bottom, twisting and turning back on themselves and biting their own tails. Between them a straight staff had been placed with two snakes that curled and wound from side to side of it, ending with their heads facing each other at the top. Each snake head was crowned with a little coronet. On top of the staff between them perched a bird, facing to the left. On the left of the staff, a sun with spiky rays was drawn. On the right of the staff was a thin crescent moon. It was a drawing of the brick pattern William had just seen on the wall above the fireplace.

Surprised, he swung the torch away from the book and shone it across the room to where the brick fireplace gaped in the far wall, with its canopy above. But no design was now visible on the worn surface. William went quickly round the table and stood in the centre of the hearth, pointing his torch up at the canopy. Then he stood on the stool to reach a little higher. He moved the torch beam backwards and forwards over the surface of the bricks. Although the wall was rough and indented in many places, where the brick had crumbled, there was no sign of any design or motif on it at all. But it had been there. Of that he was certain. It had been there and now it had vanished. What was more, the picture in the book confirmed this for him. Returning to the table, he looked again at the rough drawing. It was as though the person responsible for it had had to come back to it many times before it was completed to his or her liking. There were innumerable pale outlines of different dragons before the final two were etched in in darker strokes. The snakes climbing the staff had ghostly counterparts that had been previously rejected. Dimly, a crescent moon could just be seen on the left of the staff, placed there before the sun had been drawn over it. It was as if the artist was trying to recall precisely what had been seen when he or she was no longer in the presence of the real thing. But what had finally been settled upon was, without any doubt, the same strange design that William had seen when he was looking down from the gallery above.

William shivered. The cold in the hall was intense. But he was reluctant to go back to bed. He felt himself to be on the brink of an important discovery, if only he could understand what the picture was trying to tell him. He stared at it again. Phoebe had said that the dragons represented nature. But what did that mean? And how did she know? And what were the snakes and what was the bird and why the sun and the moon?

Then, with a gasp, William thought of something else. Or rather, he thought in a different way. Was it, perhaps, the fireplace that was important? Was the reason that the unknown artist (although, come to think of it, William told himself, the artist is almost certainly Jonas Lewis, considering that this is his book) had difficulty drawing the picture exactly the same as the one that he would now have; was it because the picture had disappeared? Then another thought occurred to him. Was the picture trying to tell him, and before him Jonas, that the secret lay . . . in the chimney?

As William had the thought, he shivered again. And then he remembered the little window in the eaves.

'Of course,' he said, aloud, and he ran back to the fireplace. But this time he went right into the hearth, so that he was standing in the opening, and shone the torch up the chimney. Above him the shaft rose, black with soot, into the dark. The beam of his torch could not penetrate the upper reaches of the chimney. The walls of the chimney seemed to be built in sections and up the back face there were protuberances, at regular intervals, as the opening gradually narrowed.

At first, William was disappointed. He had been so sure that he was right. He swept the torch beam slowly down the shaft, moving it from side to side as he did so, and then he suddenly noticed a ledge up above him, not much higher up than the height of an average man. It seemed natural that it should be there. After it, the chimney started to narrow gradually. But on the side wall, to the left, the ledge was broader than at the back or to the right.

William moved to the left of the hearth, and shone the torch straight up at the ledge. Was there, perhaps, an opening leading from it, into the back wall of the chimney? He wasn't tall enough to be sure, and the torch light was not strong enough to penetrate the deep gloom.

Just supposing, he thought, just supposing there were steps up the chimney.

He walked slowly back to the table, deep in thought. The window they had seen would be at the top of this staircase. The room that he was certain was up there would lead off it. It was a perfect hiding place.

But a hiding place for what? And why? Hiding what?

He sat on one of the chairs at the table and rested his head in his hands. He was certain that the answer was within his grasp, if he could only organize his thoughts. He had already worked out that the top floor of the tower, in other words the attic, where their bedrooms were, and where he also suspected the secret room was situated, had been added during the Tudor period. The fireplace had also been installed during that time. The two fitted together perfectly. Someone, during the reign of Henry the Eighth, or Mary, or Edward the Sixth, or Queen Elizabeth, had built on to the house. Then William recalled illustrations of Elizabethan black and white timber buildings that he had seen in a project about the age of 'Good Queen Bess'.

So, he thought, the building was added to, some time during the reign of Elizabeth the First. So what? Am I any nearer the answer to the puzzle?

He crossed round the table again and looked at Jonas Lewis's book. But that was no help. It had been written, according to the front page, in 1899. So who, in 15 . . . whenever it was that the new building had been added . . . wanted to hide a room up under the eaves?

Then William remembered that Uncle Jack had said that the envelope he had been given by the woman at the library contained a list of the people who had lived in the house.

Of course, William thought, as he opened the envelope and extracted the sheets of paper that it contained, a name isn't going to mean very much to me.

But it did. The name meant a great deal to him.

He scanned down the list of dates and names, written in a spiky longhand, until he came to:

1542. *Gelden Place stripped of religious protection and abandoned.*

1550. *The property is purchased and restored as a private dwelling, to be called Golden House. The new owner is one 'Stephen Tyler, from the City of London'.*

As William read the name he recalled the strange meeting on the platform at Druce Coven Halt, and how the tall man in the black coat with the piercing eyes and the hair the colour of a fox had held him by the shoulder.

'My name,' William heard a voice in his head saying, 'is Stephen Tyler. Will you remember that?'

William dropped the piece of paper and ran back up the staircase and into the cold but welcoming safety of his bed.

11

Morning

William awoke to discover Mary, fully dressed, sitting on the side of his bed.

'What time is it?' he asked, surprised into wakefulness.

'Nearly ten,' Mary answered.

'You should have called me sooner.'

Mary shook her head and looked at her hands.

'What's the matter, Mare?' William asked, alarmed by her behaviour.

'Phoebe's ill,' Mary told him in a low voice. 'She's staying in bed.'

'Very ill?' William asked her as he struggled into his clothes.

Mary shrugged.

'Uncle Jack says she just needs to rest. But by the way he's behaving I should think she must be very ill indeed. You'd better come down, Will.'

'Where's Alice?'

'She's in the kitchen.'

'Why didn't you call me?' William said again, as he wiped a wet flannel across his face. It was freezing cold in the bathroom and the window was piled high with snow on the outside.

'Uncle Jack said we had to let you sleep,' Mary answered.

She was standing at the bathroom door, watching him.

'What's going on, Mare? You're behaving funnily,' William said.

'Uncle Jack was really cross with us,' she said in a low voice, looking over her shoulder as if she was afraid of being overheard. 'Something to do with that book. We didn't know what he was going on about. He's going to ask you now.'

'Ask me what?'

'Oh William, did you go down in the middle of the night and look at it?'

'What if I did? No one told us not to.'

'We made a Solemn Vow, William. You broke it.'

'Yes, I know,' William admitted, as he put on his shoes. 'I'm sorry, Mare. I couldn't sleep – and I didn't want to wake you, and . . . well, I just had to know about the secret room. I'm sorry. Really I am.'

'There's no point making Solemn Vows if you just go and break them.'

'Oh, Mary!' William exclaimed. 'I've said I'm sorry.'

'Anyway, Uncle Jack's furious about it,' Mary said.

'I left the book lying open on the table in the hall,

that's how he knew. But I don't see why he should be cross about it. Last night we were all looking at it together.'

'Maybe it's just that he's worried about Phoebe,' Mary said as she led the way down the spiral stairs to the gallery below.

Dull light filtered into the great hall from the two windows on either side of the front door. As William started down the main stairs, he glanced at the canopy above the fireplace, but there was insufficient light to see if the brick picture was visible or not.

Alice was sitting on a chair beside the kitchen range. She looked small and cold and miserable. As the other two entered she pulled a face that said: I don't like it here. Let's go home! and she motioned with her head towards the back door, through which a moment later Uncle Jack entered, carrying a large basket of logs.

'Oh, you're up, are you?' he said to William, as he stamped his feet on the floor to dislodge snow from his boots. 'Well, after you've had some breakfast you can help me to get logs in, all right?'

'OK,' William answered.

'There's porridge on the range. And milk in the larder,' Jack told him. Then, before William had a chance to help himself to a bowl from the dresser, he continued:

'You came down in the night, William?'

'I couldn't sleep,' William replied.

'So it was you who looked at the book, yes?'

William shrugged.

'I didn't know it wasn't allowed.' His voice sounded indignant. He wasn't going to be blamed for something about which he didn't feel guilty. He glared defiantly at Jack.

'Well you do now,' Jack answered him after a moment. 'I've put that book away and I don't want any of you looking at it. And that's an order.'

'But why?' Alice demanded. 'It's just a book. Why can't we look at it?'

'I don't want any arguments about this,' Jack said. Then he added, rather weakly: 'It's not for children, that's all.'

'What's wrong . . . ?'

'William, I told you. I don't want any argument,' Jack cut in. 'Now the subject is closed.'

'I was only going to ask,' William said once more in the same indignant voice, 'what was wrong with Phoebe. That was all.'

'She's not feeling too good. She'll be all right,' Jack answered. 'Well, get your breakfast. There's a lot to be done today. You'll find me in the barn chopping wood when you've finished,' and he went out again to the yard, closing the kitchen door after him.

As soon as they were alone, the children drew together round the open range and started whispering all at the same time.

'Wait a minute! Shut up both of you! Please!' William interrupted them. 'We've got to stop Uncle Jack lighting a fire in the hall.'

'Oh, why, Will? I'm frozen,' Alice wailed.

But William was already hurrying towards the hall door and didn't answer her.

'Where are you going?' Mary demanded, feeling her temper rising.

'I'll explain in a minute,' he said. 'But first, one of you keep watch out of the window for Uncle Jack and the other come and tell me if he's coming back in.'

'No!' Mary said, firmly. 'We'll not do anything of the sort. I'm fed up with you bossing us about, William. You broke a Solemn Vow. There's no excuse for that. A Solemn Vow, William. None of us has ever broken one before.'

'I know and I really am sorry,' William said, pausing in the doorway and looking suitably ashamed of himself. 'I know it was wrong of me . . . but I just couldn't help myself.'

'Of course you could,' Mary snapped. 'That's the point of a Solemn Vow – to stop us doing something we want to do, because we promised each other we wouldn't. It's just like you! Just because you're older. Well I won't put up with it . . .'

'Oh, Mary!' William shouted, dangerously near to losing his temper as well. 'If I waste time arguing with you, it'll be useless,' and he ran into the hall and crossed to the fireplace.

'Where are you going?' Alice asked, following him.

'Sssh!' William hissed, glancing up at the gallery in the direction of Phoebe and Jack's bedroom. 'She's up there,' he whispered. 'Will you keep watch, Alice?'

'All right, but why, Will? Please tell us why,' Alice pleaded.

But William was lost in thought, standing in the vast fireplace. It was big enough for two narrow ledge seats along each side. Though anyone sitting on them would get horribly hot when the fire was alight, he thought. Then he noticed that, by standing on the left one, he was able to reach a protruding stone that jutted out of the wall some way above the bench. There was another stone set at a higher level and at an angle to the first. Above this second stone, a third stuck out, just below the level of the ledge he had seen by torch light the night before. The stones were big enough to stand on. They formed a rough way of climbing up to the ledge.

'I'm going up,' he whispered just as Mary, unable to bear not knowing what was going on, came out of the kitchen.

'William!' she hissed in a loud, impatient whisper. 'William, where are you going?' and she ran across the hall and into the fireplace.

At first it was too dark for her to make out anything

at all. But, as her eyes grew accustomed to the gloom, so, gradually, she was able to make out the figure of her brother, standing on a ledge above her head.

'What are you doing?' she whispered.

'I'm not sure,' William replied. 'I should have brought the torch.'

'Mary!' Alice's agitated voice sounded behind her. 'Mary!'

'What?' she asked, swinging round.

'He's coming,' her sister hissed and a moment later Uncle Jack pushed past her into the hall, carrying three large logs cradled across his arms.

Mary gasped and stepped out of the fireplace as Jack came towards her.

'Out of the way, Mary. These are heavy,' he said, and he dropped them on the stone slabs in front of the hearth.

'Where's William?' Jack asked, straightening up and wiping his hands on his jeans.

'He's gone . . .' Mary said uncertainly. She was never very good at lying.

'Gone?' Jack asked, looking at her suspiciously.

'Upstairs,' she replied and at once she felt more confident. After all, that was where he had gone, in a way. He was at least higher up than they were, so it wasn't really a lie.

Jack frowned and crossed to the kitchen door.

'Well, tell him I need help. And there's masses you

two can be getting on with in the kitchen.' Then, seeing Alice standing forlornly in front of him, he seemed to repent a little. 'Sorry,' he said, turning back to look at Mary and putting a hand on Alice's shoulder at the same time. 'I must have got out of bed the wrong side this morning.' Then he lifted up a hand, like an American Indian. 'Friends?' he said, with a smile.

Mary pursed her lips and looked at her feet.

'What d'you want us to do in the kitchen?' she said, wishing her voice didn't sound sulky.

'I thought we could get things ready for tomorrow, so that Phoebe doesn't have too much work.'

'Is she very ill?'

'No. She's just . . .' Jack shrugged. 'Well, you know what it's like being pregnant.'

'Uncle Jack!' Mary exclaimed and then she blushed.

'Well, I expect you know as much as I do about it,' Jack said and he grinned again.

'She's not going to have her baby now, is she?' Alice asked in a startled voice.

'I hope not,' Jack replied and for a moment he looked almost worried. 'No, I'm sure she isn't. She just got worked up last night . . .'

'About that book?' Mary asked and when Jack didn't reply, she continued, 'I don't see what's so special about it anyway. It's just an old book. I thought it was a bit boring, really.'

'Good,' Jack said and smiled. 'Now, I'm going to light a fire and Phoebe's coming down to sit in front of it and we're going to give *her* a good time for a change. Agreed?' and he went out into the kitchen again, without waiting for a reply.

At once Mary dashed back into the fireplace, skipping over the three big logs that Jack had placed on the hearth.

'William, William,' she called. 'Uncle Jack is going to light a fire.'

'What's going on down there?' a voice above them said, and a moment later Phoebe appeared at the top of the stairs and started to come down into the hall.

Alice stared at her in confusion and couldn't think of anything to say. Mary came out of the fireplace and looked up at her, grinning in a stupid way.

'What are you two up to?' Phoebe said, but she was smiling and sounded friendly.

'I thought you were ill, Phoebe. We were going to get everything ready for you before you came down,' said Mary, saying the first words that came into her head.

'I'm fine now. I'm going to make myself a cup of tea. Where's Jack?'

'Getting logs,' Alice said.

'And William?' Phoebe continued.

'I'm helping him make a fire,' a voice behind Mary

announced and, as they all turned to look at the fire-place, William stepped out.

'William!' Phoebe laughed. 'You're covered in soot!' It was true. William's face had smears across it, and his hands were black. 'We should have had that chimney swept. Well, there's no point in washing until you've finished the job.' Then she shivered. 'It's cold out here,' and she went into the kitchen.

As soon as they were alone, the two girls ran to William.

'Where've you been?' and 'What's happening?' they both said at the same time.

'I've found it,' William said, his eyes shining with excitement.

'What, oh what?' Alice pleaded.

'At least, I think I have.'

'Oh, William. What?' Mary's impatience was beginning to make her sound cross again.

'The way to the secret room,' and as he spoke he turned to look at the fireplace.

The two girls followed his stare.

'You mean . . .' Mary began, taking a step forward.

'Up the chimney?' Alice finished her sentence for her.

'Yes, oh yes. I think so,' William responded.

'But . . . how?' Alice said, staring at the great brick opening.

'Well, I didn't have a torch,' William began, 'and it was very dark up there but . . . I'm almost certain.'

'William!' Jack's voice was heard calling from the kitchen. 'Hurry up. I need help.'

'I'm coming, Uncle Jack,' William yelled and started towards the kitchen door.

'Not before you've told us,' Alice said, planting herself firmly in his path, her hands on hips, looking like business.

'Yes, come on, Will,' Mary agreed. 'You're being a real bore about this. What have you discovered?'

'There are steps up the chimney,' he said and he hurried past her out of the hall.

12

The Dovecote

Phoebe's arrival downstairs altered all the plans. It was decided that the fire should not be lit in the hall until the evening because it would be a waste of wood and she told the girls that she 'wouldn't dream' of letting them help her in the kitchen.

'Good gracious, you're on holiday. You don't want to spend your time cooking and washing up.'

Alice had to admit that, for a witch, she was behaving very nicely.

But, even so, they all had a busy morning and the girls didn't get a chance to discuss William's discovery with him, much as they longed to do so. They passed the time cutting holly from the bushes along the drive to decorate the hall and William spent the morning out in the barn with Uncle Jack, sawing wood and stacking it on the great mound of logs that already was housed there.

'I don't know why we needed to do any more. You'd think there'd be enough there already to see them right through till the spring,' he said later, when they were washing their hands before lunch. But when Mary pointed out that the kitchen range also used the same source of fuel he agreed that it was probably necessary and that, 'Anyway, I quite enjoyed doing it.'

'Why can't they have coal, like everybody else does?' Alice said. 'You don't have to chop coal. It comes ready to use.'

'I suppose it's a long way for the coal lorry to come. Maybe they wouldn't deliver this far out,' William suggested.

But Mary shook her head:

'I think it's more likely to be because of money,' she said. 'They're probably very poor and can't afford things like coal and central heating and all the nice things.'

'Maybe that's why they only eat vegetables,' said Alice, who was determined to get to the reason for what she considered to be by far the strangest of Phoebe's peculiarities. 'I bet if someone was to wrap up half a pound of sausages and give them to her for a Christmas present she'd gobble them all up without even waiting to cook them.'

'Ugh, Alice!' William protested. 'Uncooked sausages would be revolting.'

'Not half so revolting as stuffed cabbage leaves,' his sister replied threateningly.

'Is that what we're having for lunch?' William asked.

Alice nodded silently and then made a hideous sick noise.

'Stuffed with what, Al?' Mary asked, nervously.

Alice shrugged.

'I don't know,' she said airily. 'I didn't like to ask, did I? It looks like . . .'

'Don't tell us, Alice,' both her brother and sister cut in, and William put a hand over her mouth, to stop her saying any more.

'When will we go up the steps in the chimney?' Mary wondered aloud, as she was combing her hair. 'It'll be difficult, with Jack and Phoebe coming in and out all the time.'

'I know,' William agreed. 'It'll have to be tonight, after they're in bed.'

'In the dark?' Alice squealed.

'We've got a torch,' William told her, without sounding all that confident himself. 'And we'll be with you, Al.'

'I'm not scared,' Alice snapped. 'I just wondered, that's all,' and she ran ahead of the others down the stairs to the kitchen.

The lunch turned out to be delicious and even the dreaded stuffing tasted quite nice. It was, so Phoebe told them, 'lentils and things'. William had a second helping and Alice wanted one, only she couldn't bring herself to admit that she'd actually enjoyed it.

After lunch Jack tried to persuade Phoebe to go upstairs for a rest saying that he and the children would wash up, but once again Phoebe refused.

'They're on holiday, Jack. I'll do the washing up and then I'll have a rest.'

'All right then, you lot,' Jack said, 'in that case you can go out for a while. It's stopped snowing now and so long as you keep to the tracks you should be all right.'

'Jack, they may not want to go out.'

'Yes we will,' William said firmly just before Mary managed to agree with Phoebe.

'Good,' said Jack, with a grin, 'because I've got things that I want to get on with and I don't want you all here when I do them.'

'What sort of things?' Alice asked, surreptitiously helping herself to another shortcake biscuit.

'Christmas things,' he answered mysteriously. 'Surprise things. So off you go and get your coats and scarves and gloves and hot-water bottles and whatever else you may need. It's bitterly cold out.'

'We don't really have to take hot-water bottles outside with us, do we?' Alice asked, as they were putting on thick socks and other warm things in their rooms.

'No, of course not,' William called across the landing. 'That was his joke.'

'Well, it was a really pathetic one, if you ask me,' Mary said and then she sighed.

'What's the matter, Mare?' Alice asked her as she twisted a scarf round her neck.

'Oh, it's nothing,' Mary answered, making it sound very important indeed.

'What is it?' Alice said, suddenly really worried.

'It's just that he's so lovely. Uncle Jack, I mean. But, when he says silly things and agrees with whatever Phoebe suggests straight away and does what he's told, it makes him look so, I don't know, so . . . well, silly, really.'

'Oh Lord,' wailed Alice as William came into the room ready to go and carrying his newly acquired wellington boots.

'Now what's the matter?' he said.

'Mary's in love with Uncle Jack now,' she continued to wail.

'Oh no!' William also sounded mournful. 'She can't be.'

'I'm not,' Mary protested, blushing.

'She *is*,' William continued, looking at her.

'Shut up, William,' Mary yelled and she threw a wellington at him.

William caught the boot and grinned.

Mary ignored him and went out on to the landing and across to William's room. She stared thoughtfully at the brick wall that they now believed divided them from the secret room.

'D'you really think those steps would reach all the way up to here?' she said, thoughtfully.

But William put a finger to his lips.

'Come on,' he said in a low voice. 'We'd better talk

outside,' and he ran down the stairs, his socks making no sound on the stone steps.

The girls hurried after him and when they reached the landing, they were surprised to find Phoebe standing at the bottom of the spiral staircase.

'There you are,' she said brightly. 'Enjoy yourselves, but don't go too far. It gets dark so early at this time of year. And stay on the track . . .'

'All right, Phoebe,' William called over his shoulder and the three children ran down the stairs and out through the kitchen into the back porch, where they stopped to pull on their boots.

'You see what I mean?' William whispered. 'She was listening to us. We must be careful.'

The yard was formed by the back wall of the house, with the barn running at a right angle to it. Opposite the house, and at a right angle to the barn, a high brick wall obscured the view. In this wall there was an arch which held a wooden gate. The fourth side of the yard was open and gave a view of the drive, though even here there were signs of a fourth wall which had at some time collapsed or been pulled down.

Mary led the way across the yard towards the gate in the wall. The air was so cold that their breath smoked in front of them and the whiteness of the snow was so bright that they had to half close their eyes against the dazzle. The gate was difficult to move.

'There must be snow piled up on the other side,' Mary said. Eventually, with the help of the other two, she managed to push it open wide enough to squeeze through.

Alice went in first.

'Oh, come and look,' she called. But she needn't have bothered. The others were in before she'd finished speaking.

They were standing in a vast walled garden. There were fruit trees against the walls and others that stood in rows, their branches trained over arches and along trelliswork fences, forming walks and arbours, with seats in some and big troughs in others. There were low hedges indicating a pattern of paths that would otherwise have been obliterated by the thick covering of snow that shrouded everything in smooth white. All the paths converged on a central point and here stood a tall round building, its walls pierced by innumerable little windows, each with a ledge in front of it. There was a door in the base of this building and the children were naturally drawn towards it, both out of curiosity and also in the hope that they could step inside and shelter from the piercing wind that had sprung up as they passed through the gate and was now whipping the loose snow into a hazy cloud and sending it scudding across the surface of the ground.

The door was locked but as William rattled it the old

iron padlock clicked open and dangled on the hook.

'William. You've broken it,' Mary said.

'I never,' he protested. 'I hardly touched it.'

'What does it matter anyway? Let's get inside,' Alice said, her teeth chattering with the cold and, as she spoke, she pushed open the door and stepped through.

They were in a circular room with a stone-flagged floor. The wall above them sloped inwards.

'It's like the inside of a pudding bowl,' Mary said in a quiet voice.

Steps led up to a platform just above their heads and there were other platforms, each linked by similar steps at regular intervals right to the roof. The outer wall was pierced by the same little windows that they had seen from outside.

'What is it?' Alice asked, turning in a circle and looking up at the same time.

'A dovecote. Or a pigeon house,' William replied and he started to climb the steps to the first platform. As he did so the wood above him creaked and a shower of dust and small stones cascaded down from above.

'Be careful, Will,' Mary called. 'It doesn't look very safe to me.'

'Can I come up?' Alice asked, putting her foot on the lowest step.

'It's a bit rickety,' William said, walking carefully round the first platform.

'Can you see anything?' Mary asked.

'Lots of snow,' William replied and he started to climb up to the next platform.

'Aren't you coming, Mare?' Alice called. She was already on the first landing and was moving faster as she got more confident.

'Be careful, Alice!' Mary said and a moment later the floorboard on which Alice had just put her foot, sagged beneath her weight, dislodging a shower of dust and debris.

'Alice!' Mary cried and she started to run up the first staircase to the rescue. She found Alice pressed against the wall, with a gaping hole in the floor in front of her.

'I'm all right,' she said in a small voice and then she reached out and gripped Mary's hand.

'I say!' they heard William exclaim above them. 'Get a look at this.'

'Is it safe, William?' Mary called, anxiously.

'Yeah,' she heard him reply, but his tone didn't suggest that he was bothering much about them.

'Come on, Mare,' Alice now said more bravely, pulling at her sister's hand.

'Carefully then. These floors are all rotten and by the time we get to William, it'll be an awfully long drop.'

In fact William had reached the top platform. This was a much smaller circle than all the others, because of the sloping walls of the bell-shaped building. They found him kneeling on the floor in front of one of the little windows. The ledge was covered with litter.

'Oh, it's disgusting, William,' Mary said, wrinkling up her nose.

There were a few bones scattered about and a dead mouse amongst the mess.

'But look,' William told them, in a hushed voice.

So the girls knelt on either side of him and by pressing their faces close together they were all able to look out of the window at the same time.

The white world was outside. The garden wall was capped by a thick strip of snow and beyond it the black and white stripes of the timbered house and the grey stone tower stood out against a darkening sky.

'That's the back of the house,' William said, thinking aloud.

The girls nodded.

'So that window in the roof must be our bathroom window.'

'So?' Mary asked, straining forward, searching the distant view.

'Well? Don't you see it?'

And as he spoke, Alice let out a gasp.

'I can. I can,' she said.

'Oh, Alice! Get out of the way,' Mary exclaimed, pushing her to one side so that she wasn't blocking her view.

'Look!' whispered William and this time his voice was full of wonder.

He put his arms round the shoulders of the two girls, drawing them together so that all three of them were kneeling in a tight bunch at the window.

'Oh, look!' Mary murmured, seeing at last what was so exciting the other two.

High up on the ridge of the roof, where the roof met the brick chimneys there was a little round window, exactly the same as the one they had seen the day before at the front of the house. But this time there was a difference.

'There's a light on,' Alice said. 'There's a light on in the secret room.'

And it was true. The round window glowed with golden light. It was so bright that it was almost difficult to look at it without the brilliance hurting the eyes.

'Maybe Uncle Jack has lit the fire. Would that do it, d'you think?' Mary asked.

But William shook his head. He was about to speak when an even more surprising event made them all pull away from the opening in amazement. As they watched, a figure appeared at the distant window. They were too far away to see clearly who or what it was, but all three of them were certain of what Alice now said:

'Look! There's somebody up there.'

Then, as they continued to watch, the light at the window was blotted out by a shape that seemed to spring out of the circular opening and launch itself straight in their direction.

'What is it?' Mary cried, pulling back fearfully.

Before either of the others could reply, the answer came on its own. With a flapping of wings and a terrible screech, a great bird landed feet first on the ledge in front of them. Its talons gripped the sill and it shook its pale wings. Then it turned, slowly, and they saw its piercing eyes set in a mask-like white face.

'William,' Alice said, drawing closer to her brother.

'It's a barn owl, I think,' was all that he said.

Then, raising itself up on its stout legs, the bird suddenly hissed at them and the three children got up and ran for the stairs, tripping over each other in their anxiety to get away.

They slithered and fell and jumped and ran down from the top platform, causing showers of small stones to fall and several wooden planks to crack. Reaching the ground, they bolted for the door and didn't stop until they were halfway across the snowy garden. Then, panting and breathless, they slowed to a walk and collapsed into each other's arms, laughing and giggling.

Looking back at the dovecote, the face of the owl was framed in the upper window. It stared coldly down at them, watching them through its big dark eyes. And under its stern gaze the three children stopped laughing and grew quiet and still.

The sun was setting to the west behind the dovecote and the air was crackling with frost. But the children didn't move. They remained staring up at the owl.

'It's like the fox,' Mary said, quietly. 'It seems to . . . want us.'

'I know,' William agreed.

As if it had heard them, the owl spread its wings and launched itself on to the air. Then it sailed away silently, round the dovecote and out of their sight.

'Don't go,' Mary called and then was surprised by her own voice.

A moment later a streak of red shot from behind the dovecote and raced towards the back of the garden.

'The fox!' William exclaimed.

As he spoke, the fox stopped in its tracks, slewed round in the snow, sending up a shower of silver and white that shimmered golden in the rays of the setting sun, and stood, one paw raised, staring at them.

'It *is* the owl,' William said almost to himself.

'But how can it be?' Alice asked, but not disagreeing with him.

'I don't know. But . . . the way it looks at us . . .' William said. He started to walk slowly towards the fox, one hand held out in front of him, as though it was a dog he was trying to befriend.

The fox continued to stare, but before William had taken many steps, it turned and with a bound of immense energy it darted away down a distant path, parallel to the one they were on, making for the door in the wall.

The children hurried to follow, but by the time they reached the gate the fox was already out of sight.

'There you are!' said Uncle Jack, appearing at the kitchen door. 'We wondered what had happened to you. Come in and get warm. I've just made a pot of tea.'

As they crossed the yard, Alice suddenly stopped and grabbed Mary's arm.

'Look, Mare,' she said and she pointed to the distant trees beyond the drive.

The dog was standing on the edge of the flat land, where the steep bank of the valley started. Its tail was wagging and, as the three children stopped to look at it, it barked loudly then turned and bounded up into the obscurity of the forest.

'My dog,' Alice murmured gladly.

'Now we've seen them all. Except . . .' William didn't finish the sentence.

'Except what, Will?'

'The man. Stephen Tyler.'

'But why should we see him here?' Mary was puzzled.

'He has the same eyes, as well. The same stare.'

'Then maybe he made the footprints I found,' Alice said and then she gasped. 'And maybe . . .'

'Yes. Maybe,' William said quietly.

'Maybe what?' Mary cried.

'Maybe he can change himself into foxes and owls and dogs and . . . things,' Alice told her.

'How!' Mary protested. 'He'd have to be a magician to do that.'

'Then, maybe he is,' said William, quietly.

13

Tempers and Moods

Whatever the surprises were that Jack had been preparing, there was no sign of them when they went in. Phoebe was busy in the kitchen, making supper and also 'things for tomorrow's meal'.

Alice gave William a sideways look at this, which seemed to imply that 'things' could mean almost anything and he had to look away quickly, for fear of laughing in Phoebe's face.

They had a mug of tea sitting round the kitchen fire and then went up to their rooms to 'play until supper' as William put it, much to Mary's disgust.

'Honestly, William. We're not children,' she protested as she followed him up the stairs. Alice had run on ahead and was already kneeling in front of the electric fire when the other two came in.

'I'm frozen stiff,' she said. 'The sooner Uncle Jack lights the big fire the better.'

'Move over, Alice,' Mary said, squatting down beside her and holding her hands out to the glowing bar.

William stood at the window, his hands in his trouser

pockets, staring out at the almost night sky. The two girls glanced at him and then exchanged a look.

'He's thinking,' Mary whispered, pulling a face.

'Shut up, Mary,' he said, without looking at them.

Alice started to giggle and Mary put a hand over her mouth and then she also felt a sudden urge to laugh. The two girls tried hard not to let this show but eventually they were rolling on the floor, shaking and groaning with the pain in their stomachs from holding back the laughter.

William remained standing at the window, a frown on his brow as he concentrated on the events of the day, seemingly oblivious to them. Eventually he arrived at a decision and without a word he turned and went out of the room.

'Where are you going?' Alice called, scrambling up and following him.

'To my room. I think we should have an early night tonight. We should come to bed as soon as supper is over . . .'

'You mean so we can get up later,' Alice interrupted, 'and go up the chimney?'

'No, I think we should leave that for another night. I'm really tired.'

'Well, I'm not going straight to bed.' Mary now joined Alice in the protest. 'Uncle Jack is going to light the fire in the hall.'

'Well, there won't be any point, will there? If we're all going to bed.'

'But if we're not going up the chimney, I want to sit by the fire,' Mary insisted.

'Why?' William demanded. 'What will be so special about that?'

'It'll be nice,' Mary answered. 'We can sit there and . . .' She couldn't think of anything spectacular to add, and so she just shrugged. 'Well, we can just . . . enjoy it.'

'Exactly. We can just sit there. That's all. Well, I've got more important things to do. So I'm going to bed early.'

'Honestly, William!' Mary snapped, giving him a pity-ing look. 'You must think we're thick or something.'

William turned away, not wanting to meet her eyes.

'Why?' Alice squealed. 'What's going on? What d'you mean, Mary?'

'He's going to go up the chimney on his own,' Mary told her.

'When?' Alice demanded, indignantly.

'Tonight, of course,' Mary replied.

'Without us? He can't. William Constant, we made a Solemn Vow. You've already broken it once. If you go without us, I'll never believe in you again. Not ever.'

'Oh, all right,' William snapped, giving in with bad grace. 'I'll come and get you.'

'But why in the middle of the night?' Alice wailed. 'I'm sure there'll be ghosts here.'

'Either we go then or not at all,' William told her. 'It's Christmas tomorrow, Alice.'

'I know that,' Alice said, sounding cross.

'Well, the fire'll be alight and Phoebe and Jack'll be there . . .'

'William,' Mary announced in a firm voice, 'if you go up the chimney without us, we'll never forgive you and we'll make your life really miserable. That's a promise.'

'I've said I'll come for you,' William groaned, 'but you'll only be scared.'

'No more scared than you'll be,' Mary retorted. 'Of course we'll be scared. But we've got to go together – or at least you've got to give us the chance to . . .'

'Yes, I've said I will,' William replied. 'Now clear off. I want to get out of these clothes.'

'Oooh!' Mary exclaimed, kicking the floor and walking back across the landing to the girls' room. 'Stuck-up pig. I hate him when he gets like this.'

'He's right, though. I will be scared. Oh, Mary, just think, it's Christmas Eve. If Mum and Dad were here and we were at home in London . . . what would we be doing now?'

'Oh, shut up, Alice,' Mary said, glumly.

'Supper in front of the tree and then the midnight service. Coming home all frosty and tired and hot water bottles in the beds. Oh, I wish they were here.'

'You don't even like church,' Mary said, brushing her hair and staring in the mirror.

'I do,' Alice protested. 'So long as they don't go on too much. I like the songs . . .'

'Hymns, Alice,' Mary said in a show-off sort of voice.

'And Hers, then,' Alice snapped back. 'It's sexist otherwise. I don't like the long palms.'

'Psalms,' Mary told her.

'You shut up, Mary. What does it matter if I get the words wrong?'

'If you get the words wrong, how can you expect anyone to know what you're trying to say?'

Alice shrugged and closed her eyes.

'I won't speak ever again then,' she said, and she pinched her lips together.

It was a bad-tempered and disgruntled group that gathered round the kitchen table for supper and the atmosphere was not helped by Phoebe saying that she felt sick soon after the food was on the table and Uncle Jack taking her up to bed and leaving the children to look after themselves.

Alice hummed to herself and ate great quantities of cauliflower cheese. She always hummed when she was in a 'not speaking' mood. William stared at his plate and refused to be drawn into any conversation by Mary, who eventually got so annoyed that she pushed her plate away from her and banged her fists on the table in fury.

'I'm fed up, fed up, fed up,' she said. A statement which received silence from William and an increase in the volume of the tuneless humming from Alice.

Eventually Jack returned, looking worried.

'I hope she's all right,' he said. 'I wouldn't be able to get her to the hospital, not through this snow.'

Jack was therefore relieved when William announced with a great deal of yawning that he was so tired he didn't want to sit up after supper, but that he would go straight to bed, if that was all right.

'Maybe it would be best,' Uncle Jack said. 'Not much point lighting the fire if we're all going to bed in half an hour. What do you girls say?'

Alice shrugged and looked at her plate. Since Jack's return she had stopped humming, but she was still 'not speaking'.

Mary, however, wasn't prepared to give in so easily.

'Maybe we could sit by the kitchen fire,' she said. 'It is Christmas Eve after all, Uncle Jack.'

'All the more reason to go to bed early,' he told her, trying to sound cheerful. 'Otherwise you might catch Father Christmas doing the rounds.'

'Oh, please!' she said. 'We are *not* children.'

'Sorry,' Jack said, looking suitably shamefaced.

Mary stared at him through slitty eyes. She had a feeling that he was teasing her. If he was, then that would be the final insult of the horrible evening they were having.

Jack grinned at her. It looked as though he was making a face, though actually he was trying to be friendly.

Right, thought Mary, you'll wish you weren't teasing me.

'Aren't you going to marry Phoebe, Uncle Jack?' she asked in an innocent voice, watching the surprise hit him like a slap in the face.

'What?' he gasped.

'Aren't you going to marry her? Particularly now, with the baby coming. Poor thing,' she added and she stretched across the table to help herself to a tangerine. William was watching her, horrified, and Alice's mouth had dropped open for the first time in ages, apart from the necessity of admitting food.

'Marry her? Oh, I see. Well, yes, we . . . we may,' Jack stammered.

'Why haven't you, though?' Mary pressed her point.

'Well, because . . . has this really got anything to do with you, Mary?' Jack asked, trying to sound adult and therefore superior to her.

'I only asked,' Mary said, still innocent and sweet. 'It seems such a pity that the baby'll be born out of wedlock.'

'Mary!' William protested.

'What? We've all been talking about it. What's so awful about me asking?'

'Nothing,' Jack said, regaining his composure. 'We

just haven't married yet in a legal sense. But we feel very much married to each other – in spirit.'

'But you haven't been to church, have you?' Mary pressed on. 'Nor even to a registry office.'

'But we never go to church. It'd be hypocritical to go just to get married! And I loathe the idea of a registry office.'

'You'd think she'd have wanted a nice wedding. Even if you don't.'

'I promise you something. When we get married, *if* we get married, it will be the most beautiful wedding,' Uncle Jack said, 'and you will all be invited. All right?'

Mary shrugged.

'It'll be a bit late then, won't it?' she said.

'Don't be such a little prude, Mary!' Jack laughed. 'And it wasn't me that didn't want to get married yet. It was both of us. So please don't think I'm some horrible person stopping Phoebe from having her heart's desires.' Now he sounded a little angry.

'Oh, I don't. Honestly I don't, Uncle Jack,' Mary said, very contrite. 'Please don't think that,' and she had to stop talking for fear of beginning to cry.

William sighed and Alice started to hum. Jack looked embarrassed and Mary got up from the table and with a mumbled 'I think I'll go to bed now,' she ran from the room.

'Oh dear,' said Uncle Jack when the door closed.

'She'll be all right,' William told him. 'She gets in these states.'

'But what caused it?' Jack said, utterly confused.

William and Alice exchanged a look but remained silent.

And so the day came to an early close. William and Alice said good night to Jack, who said that he'd just do the washing-up and then he also would go to bed.

'I couldn't tell him she was in love with him, could I?' Alice said as she and her brother climbed the stairs to bed.

'Love!' William exclaimed. 'Honestly!' and he sounded far from sympathetic.

As they parted on the landing Alice said:

'Why must we go to bed? I'm not even tired. We could go up the chimney now. Why not? Oh, let's, Will . . .'

But William silenced her with a gesture and looked over his shoulder down the dark well of the spiral staircase.

'Sssh, Alice!' he hissed.

'Oh, Will, there's so much to talk about; so much has happened today. The owl and the window . . . We actually saw somebody at the window of the secret room . . .'

'Shut up, Alice. You never know who might be listening. Go to bed. I'll come for you later.'

'But why not *now*?' Alice insisted in a lower voice.

'Because!' he answered, sounding cross again. 'Oh,

Alice! Don't keep asking questions! Jack's still up for one thing. And . . . oh, just leave it to me. I am the oldest, you know.' And, without waiting for any more conversation, he went into his room and closed the door.

Alice went thoughtfully into the girls' room. Mary was lying on her side in bed, with her eyes closed. She looked miserable and tense. Alice crossed and sat on the edge of her bed.

'Stuck-up pig!' she exclaimed. 'You're right, Mary. I hate William when he's like this. Mary! Mary – you're not asleep . . .'

'What?' Mary said, her face half covered with the eiderdown.

'William's still acting like a stuck-up pig!'

But Mary continued to ignore her. So Alice got undressed and climbed into bed without speaking to her again. Instead, she said aloud to herself:

'It's been a perfectly horrid evening and I wish I was an only child.'

The overhead light had been left on and the switch was by the door. Each girl waited for the other to get out and cross the cold room to switch it off. Neither of them moved. Eventually Alice fell asleep.

Well, I'm not going to do it, Mary thought and then she fell asleep as well.

14

The Steps up the Chimney

William woke with a start. It was dark in the room but his first thought was that he had overslept. He switched on the torch and looked at his watch. It was six o'clock. He had meant to be awake earlier.

He got out of bed quickly and pulled on his clothes in the dark. Luckily he'd brought his gym shoes with him, so he'd be able to move about easily and without any noise. Taking the torch, he crept out on to the landing.

Light glowed under the girls' door.

He pushed it open gently and went in. Because of the light, he thought he'd find them awake and waiting for him. But they were both asleep. He crossed the room and shook Mary.

'Mary,' he whispered, 'Mary, wake up!'

But Mary only grunted and pulled away from him.

'Wake up!' he hissed in her ear.

'Go away, Will,' she said, in a sleepy voice.

He looked round at Alice, fast asleep with her cheek on her hand. Then he shrugged. He'd promised to come for them. Well, he had done, he thought. It wasn't his fault if they wouldn't wake up.

Turning, he tiptoed back towards the door. He hadn't wanted to take them anyway. He'd be much better off on his own, he thought. So he went back on to the landing and ran swiftly and silently down the stone spiral to the gallery below.

The hall was in darkness. William hurried down the broad staircase. The treads were made of oak and some of the boards creaked loudly as he stood on them. Several times he glanced up at Jack and Phoebe's room, expecting the door to open and his uncle to come out to see who was moving about so early in the morning. It was only a short distance from the foot of the stairs to the fireplace but by the time he reached it his heart was beating so fast and so loudly that he had to pause, gasping for breath.

Switching on the torch again, he pointed the beam up the chimney. A cold current of air fanned his face and the wind moaned in the black vault above him. Slowly he lowered the torch until it was shining at the stones that protruded like a ladder up the side wall as far as the ledge.

Taking a deep breath to give himself courage and setting his face in a determined expression, he climbed up to the ledge.

He found the steps almost at once. They were set into

a dark niche at the back of the chimney. Here, the back wall jutted out, forming a false corner. From down below, at hearth level, it was impossible to see that this corner had a narrow passage running behind it. Indeed, even standing on the ledge, the niche was not very obvious unless, of course, you knew what you were looking for.

It was a narrow opening. William had to stand sideways in order to squeeze between the true side wall of the chimney and the thick stone protuberance formed by the false corner. The steps were situated between it and the wall. They were steep and extremely narrow, a tight little spiral twisting up into the dark so precipitously that the easiest way to climb them was by using hands as well as feet, rather like going up a ladder.

William started to climb, holding the torch in one hand and supporting himself on the upper steps with the other. Above him the roof was formed by the steps which moments later would be beneath his feet. The walls pressed close, the air was dank and stale. Pausing to adjust his grip on the torch, he was overwhelmed by the dull, throbbing silence that surrounded him. It was a little bit like being buried alive, he thought, and he started to climb again with more urgency, pushing the feeling of panic to the back of his mind with the renewed activity.

Later, as he rounded yet another twist of the stairs he found his way blocked by a narrow door, the wood black and heavily embossed with iron nails. At first, the iron latch was hard to move and then when it did it clicked so loudly that the sound was deafening in the unreal silence.

As William leaned his weight against this door, it swung slowly open on creaking hinges. Stepping through, he hoped to find that he had reached the top of the tower, but instead ahead of him more of the same stairs twisted on up into the dark. He had only taken a few steps when a resounding slam made him look round in alarm. He returned and found the door closed once more across the stairwell. Shining his torch over the rough surface of the wood he saw that there was no latch on the side of the door that now faced him.

He was trapped.

Mary woke up suddenly. One moment she had been dreaming about being a dancer who hadn't learned the right steps and the next, she was wide awake in the bedroom at Golden House.

Alice was sitting on the side of her bed, pulling on a sock.

'What time is it?' Mary asked, looking at the dark night sky outside the window.

'Ssssh!' Alice hissed. Then she whispered: 'It's quarter past six.'

'Where are you going?' Mary whispered.

'Will isn't in his room.'

'He's gone without us!' Mary exclaimed, immediately bad-tempered. 'The little beast. I knew he would. I knew it. Right, that does it . . .'

'We've got to find him, Mary,' Alice cut in, interrupting her sister's anger.

'Find him?' Mary sneered. 'I don't care where he is. I hope he gets really lost.'

'No, Mary. You don't. Not really.'

'Yes, I do. He promised us . . .'

'But he's in danger, I know he is. We've got to find him . . .'

'Serves him right if he is in danger,' Mary said. 'He's gone off alone to find the secret room and, what's more, he's broken another Solemn Vow. It's typical of him – just because he's the oldest he thinks he can do whatever he likes . . .'

'Mare,' Alice pleaded, 'he shouldn't go there on his own. It isn't safe. You said yourself there's something really funny about this place. Please come with me . . .'

And she looked so desperate and so miserable that Mary hadn't the heart to say no.

'Oh, all right,' she said, climbing out of the bed and immediately shivering. 'Oh! It's freezing in here.'

'Get dressed then,' Alice told her and she pulled the covers off Mary's bed, just in case she had any idea of returning to its warmth.

'Where are we going to look anyway?' Mary said, dressing quickly to escape the ice cold of the bedroom.

'Up the chimney, of course.'

'I don't want to go up the chimney,' Mary wailed in disgust. 'It'll be filthy.'

'What does that matter?' Alice said and already she was running out of the room.

With a sigh Mary finished dressing. I'll have to follow her, she thought, otherwise she'll only get into trouble as well as Will, and that'll make things even more complicated. What a nuisance they are . . .

As she followed Alice down the dark stairs, Mary wished that William hadn't commandeered the only torch.

William had taken his belt off and was trying to slide the prong of the buckle between the side of the door and the frame in the hope that he could move the latch on the other side. It was a good idea and it kept almost working, but because the door opened towards him and there was no handle or knob on his side he was unable to get a proper hold.

Eventually, bothered and frustrated by failure, he turned and proceeded up the spiral stairs until he reached a narrow landing with a door at the end. Pushing this door open, he stepped through it into a long moonlit loft.

'Well, come in. Come in,' a voice said, rather crossly, from somewhere in the shadows.

This took William so by surprise that instead he stepped backwards out of the room into the dark of the landing. A moment later a soft whirring sound, followed by a draught and something cold brushing his forehead, made him turn tail and run helter-skelter down the stairs, dropping his torch as he went and thus plunging himself into complete darkness.

Alice and Mary reached the door on the stairs just as William arrived at the other side of it and, feeling in the dark, Alice found the latch and pushed it open in time to be met by William running in the opposite direction. They collided and Alice fell backwards, hitting Mary who was a few steps behind her. Mary steadied herself against the stone wall and managed to stay on her feet, but Alice collapsed, with William on top of her.

'What's going on?' Mary hissed.

'I'm being suffocated,' Alice's muffled voice announced.

'Alice?' William said, trying to stand up.

'William? Is that you?' Mary whispered, feeling in front of her and contacting the muddle of bodies that was sorting itself out into William and Alice.

'What are you doing?' an irritable voice asked. It seemed to come from behind them, higher up the stairs.

'Who said that?' Alice whispered.

'I don't know,' William moaned. 'There's somebody up there.'

'Oh, do come up, if you're going to,' the voice said again. And then it added a strange 'ooo-ooo' sound, as though whoever was speaking had suddenly had a fit of the shivers.

'William, who is it?' Mary whispered, her voice quaking with fear.

'Well, there's only one way to find out,' the voice replied. 'Do come up. I won't eat you. I've had my supper and you'd be far too tough.'

'You're not to lock us in then,' William called into the darkness, trying to sound brave.

'Lock you in? Of course not. It is perfectly easy to open if you simply know how. Are you coming? I'll give you some light . . .' and, as the voice said the words, the narrow stairwell was suffused with a pale, silvery glow.

In this half light the children looked at one another. It would be possible for them to hurry down the stairs and away from the strange voice for they were standing in the open doorway.

William felt that the decision ought to be unanimous. He didn't want to be responsible for leading the girls into danger. He wasn't even sure that he wanted to go himself. He therefore whispered:

'What should we do?'

Alice pulled a face and said nothing. But Mary, to the surprise of the others, called out indignantly:

'It's all very well you telling us to do this and do that. We don't know who you are. It might be dangerous.'

'But you were going to come up, weren't you? That's why you're here,' the voice said in a patient tone. 'What is the difference now?'

'The difference,' said Mary firmly, 'is that you are there, and we don't know who you are.'

'Would it really make any difference if you did know?' the voice asked.

'Yes, it would,' Mary replied.

'Well, there's only one way to find out,' the voice said, crossly, and a moment later there was a strange, dull beating sound, followed by silence.

'Hello?' William called. The silence remained.

'Let's go back to bed,' Alice said.

'No,' Mary said, pushing past her. 'You two go, if you want, but I'm going up.'

'You're very brave, Mary,' William told her as she squeezed past him.

'I'm not really,' she whispered. 'But if he'd been going to do something awful . . . well, he'd have done it by now, wouldn't he? And besides I couldn't go back to bed now. The curiosity would kill me. Come on, you two. I don't really want to go on my own.'

'All right,' Alice said in a small, reluctant voice. 'But William, you must hold my hand very tight and promise not to let it go.'

In the half light, William reached down the stairs and took hold of the small hand. He was as glad of it as his sister was of his and wasn't surprised when Mary reached down to him from above and held firmly on to his other one.

So the three of them, hand in hand, mounted the steep stairs until they reached the moonlit chamber at the top.

15

Meeting a Magician

'Hello?' Mary called, making the word sound like a question. 'Are you there?'

There was no answer.

'Oh, come on,' said Alice, pulling at William's hand. 'If there's no one here, we may as well go.'

But Mary had already moved into the room, and was looking round in the half light.

'I wonder where it comes from,' she said. 'The light, I mean. There aren't any windows . . .' Then, as she turned to look at William and Alice, she gasped.

William, thinking that she'd seen someone standing behind him, shot forward into the room, dragging Alice, who was still clinging to his hand, with him.

'What?' he exclaimed, failing totally to hide the panic he was feeling.

Alice cowered behind her brother and put her hands over her eyes – a trick she had first adopted when she was very small.

'Look,' Mary said, pointing above their heads.

William turned and Alice, still leaning against him, turned with him.

'What is it, Will? What is it?' she asked in a frightened voice.

'The owl,' William replied, quietly. 'It's all right, Alice. It's quite safe to look.'

The door through which they had entered was set into a stone turret of what would once have been the roof of the tower. Beside it the brickwork of the chimney disappeared through the slanting gable. Where the roof joined the chimney, the two round windows that they had seen from the ground jutted out, one at the front and the other at the back. They were bigger than they had seemed from ground level, and each of them had a circular reflecting mirror fixed to the brick chimney in a direct line with it. These mirrors were on swivels, and could be turned so that they would reflect the light of the sun or the moon. Each mirror also had a candle holder fixed to it – presumably so that, if there were no sun shining or no moon, it would still be possible for light to be directed out through the circular openings in the roof.

And yet it wasn't these windows with their elaborate mirrors that had prompted Mary's cry of surprise.

It was the owl.

He was perched on the candle sconce of the window at the front of the house – the one that looked out over the drive and the high bank of woods. He was silent and still; staring solemnly out through the window, with the moonlight shining in the mirror behind him, so that he seemed to be ringed by silver light. The window was half open, tilting inwards at the top and outwards at the bottom, from a central point on each side of the circular frame. A faint breeze stirred through the room and fanned their faces. It moved the soft downy feathers on the bird's chest. It was a cold breeze and it made the children shiver.

'It's freezing,' Mary said, without really meaning to.

'Ssssh!' the bird hissed and he raised one talon, as though in a gesture.

Alice pulled in closer to William and he put an arm round her shoulders.

Then, as they continued to watch, the light of the moon faded and the room grew dark.

'Wait,' a voice whispered.

In silence the children peered at the great bird, now no more than a vague shadow, seated on the sconce above their heads. Then, almost imperceptibly at first, a few birds began to sing out in the snow-covered woods and little by little the darkness thinned into the first glimmers of early dawn.

'Ooo-ooo,' the owl fluted, loud and thrilling to the children, standing so close beside him.

Majestically he spread his huge wings and, flapping them, almost as if he were shaking them out, he hopped from the sconce to the sill of the window. For a moment they saw him, poised against the dawn and then, without looking back, he was gone, sailing away out of their sight down below the line of the roof.

'I haven't got long,' a voice behind them said, making them swing round in unison.

There in front of them stood a man in a long black cloak. He was bareheaded and he leaned heavily with one hand on a thin silver pole. It was the sort of rod you see bishops and other high-up clergymen carrying in church. But this one didn't have a cross on top of it; instead it had two dragons winding round each other with their heads thrown back and their mouths open. From the centre of each mouth a tiny silver tongue protruded with a forked tip.

As the light increased in the room, so the children were able to see him more clearly. He was almost bald and what little hair remained was red so that the man's head seemed to be surrounded by a circle of fire. But it was his eyes that were the most startling thing about him. They were a very pale blue-grey, almost white, but flecked with gold, so that they appeared to flash and blaze like the embers of a fire in the half light. And all the time they stared with such unblinking directness, as though they could see right into each of the children's minds.

Alice gripped hold of William's hand and moved closer to him, and Mary, who had been brave, now took a step back, showing her own nervousness.

For a long time there was silence in the room, as the man stared at each of them in turn, closely inspecting them. Then he nodded thoughtfully.

'You know who I am?' he asked, quietly.

'A magician,' Mary whispered.

'Yes, that certainly,' the man answered her. 'But more than that. Who am I?'

'Stephen Tyler,' William mumbled, finding it almost impossible to speak at all.

'Good. You remembered,' the man said. And he nodded again, slowly and thoughtfully.

'Who?' Alice asked William, but without for a moment taking her eyes off the man.

'The man at the railway station. The one I told you about,' William whispered.

'The one you didn't think existed,' the man now said.

'Well, I did,' Alice said, feeling braver. 'Only you disappeared before we got a chance to see you.'

'You are Alice,' the man said, silencing her. 'And you' – he swivelled his eyes round – 'are Mary.'

Mary nodded and swallowed, uncomfortable under the cold stare.

'It took you a long time to get here,' the man now said and as he did so he walked slowly away from them towards the end of the room.

'We've only been here a few days,' William protested.

'Of course,' Stephen Tyler said. 'And yet I have been waiting for longer than that.'

'Do you live up here?' Mary asked, looking round at the cluttered room which was now taking shape in the growing light.

'Live? Here? Don't ask questions,' the man snapped. Then he seemed to regret his irritation and he smiled at her. 'Wait, and you'll discover everything you need to know. Questions can be a waste of time. Not the right questions, of course. The right questions save time. So – ask the right question and you'll get an answer.'

'But how will we know what is a right question and what isn't?' Alice asked.

The man looked at her and only smiled.

'We'll know – if we get an answer,' William said, still staring at the man.

'Good,' the man said, smiling and looking pleased. Then he stared at William closely and frowned. 'You're younger than I thought,' he said and he shook his head. 'Well, no harm in that.' Sometimes he seemed to be talking more to himself than to them. 'Now, you are going to be here during the coming year? Is that right?' he asked, speaking to them all.

'Off and on,' William replied. 'We have to go away to school. But during the holidays we'll be here, I expect.'

'Our mother and father have gone to Africa,' Mary volunteered.

'Yes, yes.' Stephen Tyler waved a hand, silencing her. 'The boy told me. Mmmh.' As he made this long, thoughtful sound he turned slowly looking at them once more under furrowed brows. 'Are you constant, you three children?'

'That's our name,' Alice cried.

'But are you really constant?' the man insisted. 'Are you resolute in mind and in purpose? Are you loyal and trustworthy? Well, are you?' This last question he fired at Alice, and as he did so he jutted his head at her, peering into her eyes, making her dodge back behind William as though she'd been hit.

'I don't know,' she whispered. 'It's just our name. Constant is our name.'

'But how did you come by it?' Stephen Tyler asked her.

Alice shrugged and pouted her lower lip. She had an awful feeling that she was about to cry.

'I don't know,' she said, tremulously. 'We got it off our father, like most people get their names.'

'But your family must once have earned the name. To be called "Constant" is a great tribute. I can only hope that you are still worthy of it. To be constant means to be true and loyal. To be constant means to honour the vows that you make at all times.'

As he finished speaking he turned slowly and looked at William with his flashing, searching eyes.

William couldn't look into those eyes. He hung his

head with shame, remembering how he had broken the Solemn Vow he had made with his sisters.

'I'm sorry,' he mumbled. 'I did try to wake them, but they were asleep and Mary told me to go away. She did, honestly.'

'Doesn't matter, Will,' he heard Mary whisper and he was glad to feel her hand take his and hold it in a reassuring grip.

'A word of advice, William Constant,' the man now said, 'never make a vow unless you mean to keep it and are capable of doing so. All right?'

William nodded and was relieved when Stephen Tyler turned away. He was shaking his head and suddenly seemed very tired.

'Ask questions now,' he said in a quiet voice, with his back to them. 'But – think before you speak.'

'Are you . . .' William started and then he had to stop and clear his throat, he was still so nervous. 'Please,' he started again, 'are you related to the Stephen Tyler who made this house during the reign of Elizabeth the First? I mean – was he your ancestor?'

The man turned again and looked at him. Then he shook his head.

'It's such an unusual name, you'd think you would be,' William stammered.

'Are you really a magician?' Alice asked.

The man nodded.

'Can you turn yourself into a dog?' she continued.

'A good question,' Stephen Tyler replied. 'The answer to which is – no, not exactly.'

'Well, I don't think that's much of an answer,' Alice told him, then she dodged back behind William again, as the man frowned and made a sound in the back of his throat like a great dog growling.

'Alice,' William hissed, warning her not to provoke the man further.

'Sorry,' his sister said, hurriedly. 'But the dog – my dog – the dog outside . . . you do know him, don't you? I think you do, you have the same sort of eyes as him.'

'Yes, I know the dog you mean,' Stephen Tyler replied. 'But I don't turn myself into him, it doesn't work like that. The dog remains himself but I . . . sometimes see through him. I enter him. I live through him, you could say. Is that a better answer?'

Alice frowned and rubbed the end of her nose, a sure sign that she was confused.

'Do you understand me, little girl?' Stephen Tyler insisted.

'I expect I will, if you give me time,' she replied, then she nudged William to say something – anything – to stop the man asking her any more questions.

'Do you enter in the fox sometimes, then?' William asked.

'Sometimes the fox, yes,' Tyler replied.

'And the owl?' Mary asked.

'The owl and I are very close,' he told her.

'But . . . how?' Alice asked in a puzzled voice.

'Ah.' Stephen Tyler sighed. 'It took years of practice. I'll show you sometime.'

'Would we be able to?' Mary asked him.

'With my help,' the Magician replied. 'With my help there's no knowing what you might not accomplish.'

'And would you help us?' Alice asked, her eyes wide with wonder as she peeped round William's shoulder.

'If it's necessary, then yes, of course.'

'Necessary for what?' William asked, feeling bolder.

'Good questions,' Stephen Tyler said, beaming. 'You're all coming on very nicely. Necessary for my work.'

'What is your work?' William asked.

'Alchemy,' Stephen Tyler replied.

'You mean you can make gold out of tin?' William cried out excitedly.

'No,' Stephen Tyler said, swinging round, his eyes flashing and raising his staff as though he would beat William with it.

William cowered back, afraid and shocked by this reaction.

'But I thought that's what alchy-whatever-it-is was for,' he protested.

'Yes, people do. There was a man here – Lewis? Was that his name?'

'Jonas Lewis?' William prompted him.

'That was it. Very good. How did you know it?'

'Uncle Jack brought back a book written by him. That's how we discovered the steps up the chimney. There were drawings in it. One of them – a sun and a moon on either side of that stick you're holding . . . sometimes you can see it on the chimney piece.'

'The secret signs. Because the art is so . . . carefully guarded, we cannot just let anyone enter.' Stephen Tyler smiled. 'You did well to see it. Good, good. Very good. I'm pleased. What were we talking about?'

'Jonas Lewis,' William prompted again, feeling pleased that he'd been praised.

'Ah, yes,' Tyler continued, more quietly. 'Jonas was an apt pupil. I taught him well, of course. But he learned quickly. He was coming along very nicely. Then he got into trouble.' The old man shook his head, remembering. 'He got into trouble, and yet he didn't come to me for advice.' He shook his head again and, when he continued speaking, the tone was more brusque and business-like. 'A man called Crawden demanded payment of a gambling debt. Poor Lewis, he gambled – cards, if my memory serves me – in order to finance his alchemical explorations. I told him . . . but he wouldn't listen to me . . .'

Tyler was silent for a moment. When he next spoke, his voice had a peculiarly tragic note.

'He used the Art to make gold for himself. He paid off his debts. He thought he was free . . .'

'What happened to him?' Mary asked.

'What always happens, in the end, when we work for selfish ends. The gold reverted. It became worthless. Crawden took the house. I never saw Lewis again.'

'Were you angry with him?' Mary asked.

'Angry? Why?'

'In the book,' William told him, 'he says, "The Magus knows." He was obviously very frightened . . .'

'And Uncle Jack says,' Mary cut in, 'that a Magus is a Magician . . .'

'I was angry, yes,' the old man sighed.

'Are you really a magician?' Alice asked, with wide eyes.

Again Stephen Tyler studied them thoughtfully.

'I can turn tin into gold, if that's what you mean,' he said, at last. 'But what is the point of that? If I turned all the tin in the world into gold – then tin would be more highly valued than gold is now. The balance would change, that is all.'

'Then please,' Mary said, 'what is it that you do?'

'It is true that the alchemist's art includes the changing of base material into gold, but this is only a step on the way to the greater work.' Stephen Tyler shook his head and waved his arms in a gesture of irritation. 'The words I will have to use for you are too simple to encompass the true art. Yet some of it you must know, if you are to help me.'

'You want us to help you?' William asked, surprised by the idea.

'Of course,' Stephen Tyler replied. 'That is why I brought you here.'

'You brought us?' William said, indignantly. 'I like that. I worked it out for myself. It was me that found the steps up the chimney.'

'But it was me that built the chimney, William,' the Magician said. 'Think of that.'

'Then you are . . .' William began, then he stopped – for what he was thinking was impossible. 'You're having us on,' he said, crossly.

'How can we help you?' Mary asked, cutting in quickly. She knew how pigheaded William could be and she didn't think this was the right moment for him to start an argument – and certainly not with a magician.

'I'll let you know, when the time is right.'

'But help you doing what?' Alice demanded. It seemed to her that they were never being given any proper answers.

'A great work,' the Magician replied. 'I can't do it all on my own. I'll need some support. Particularly in your time. You need me. But at the same time, I need you, I suppose. Therefore, it's essential that we work together.'

'Work together?' William exclaimed.

'What sort of work?' Mary asked.

'Work for the future . . . Even your future. Work for mankind.'

'You mean like saving the world or something?' Alice asked. She was getting bored now and was only joking.

'Brilliant girl,' the Magician cried out. 'That's precisely what I mean. Before it's too late we must save all the worlds.'

Alice looked at William and pulled a long face. The man was obviously potty, she thought.

'You think so?' he asked her, severely, reading her mind.

'Oh, that's really mean, doing that,' Alice protested. 'Listening to our thinking. It's rude and besides we can't do it to you, so it isn't fair. It's like cheating . . . or something.'

'Alice. Shut up,' William warned her.

But he was too late, the Magician was furious. He turned on them and, holding his silver staff horizontally in front of him, he ran at them, hissing and roaring and making the most awful noise.

The children turned and ran away from him, back across the room towards the stair door through which they had entered. But just before they reached it, they heard a strange and terrifying sound. It was like a high-pitched squeak, a bit like chalk scratching on a blackboard. Before they had time even to wonder what could have made such a sound the answer came to them, in the form of a huge and hideous rat which leaped over their heads and landed in front of them, teeth bared and hissing viciously.

William was the first to scream. Later he would deny it, but that is the truth, though the girls took only a moment longer to join him.

'Oh, William!' Mary shrieked, turning and running back into the depths of the room away from the terrible creature.

Alice, meanwhile, stopped dead in her tracks and put her hands over her eyes.

'Has it gone? Has it gone?' she kept repeating in a high, frightened voice.

The rat was the biggest imaginable. It had sleek grey hair and a long shining tail that swished and twitched and was never still. It had tiny, piercing eyes that glared like pin-pricks of light.

'So,' it hissed at them, 'you're going to be tested, are you?'

And, as it finished speaking, it ran straight at Mary and round behind her, clearing the children's way to the door and at the same time forcing them to run away from it out of the room and down the steep, spiralling stairs into the darkness.

'Come on, Ally,' Will yelled, grabbing her hand and dragging her away from the room.

'Where is it? Where is it?' she wailed as she allowed

herself to be pulled down the narrow stairs into the black.

'Ssss!' hissed the rat in the darkness. 'You're going to be tesssted.'

And, further down the stairs, Alice could be heard saying:

'If there's one thing I'm really terrified of, it's *rats*.'

16

Rats

It was cold on the stairs and terribly dark. Mary, who was leading the way, came to the door first.

'Oh, William,' she shouted, 'how does it open?'

A moment later William, still dragging Alice by the hand, arrived behind her, breathing heavily.

'I don't know,' he said, desperately. 'There isn't a latch this side.'

'Oh, be quick!' Alice wailed. 'I'm sure it's following us.'

'Sssh!' William hissed, making them silent, so that they could listen.

At first there was no sound except their own breathing in the dark but then, up above them, they heard a padding, scratching sort of sound, as if someone was rubbing the fingers of each hand rhythmically across a rough surface.

'What is it?' Alice hissed, when she could bear the suspense no longer.

'I'm not sure,' William answered, but without much conviction.

'It's rat feet on the stairs,' Mary wailed. 'It is, isn't it? Oh, it is. I'm sure it is.'

'Oh, somebody get us out, please,' Alice shrieked, and then her words turned into a short scream. 'Something touched my leg,' she howled and, as she did so, she jumped up on to William's back with her arms round his shoulders and her legs round his waist.

'Alice!' William protested, then he also cried out in shock. 'There's something crawling about on the ground,' he whispered.

'I think I'm going to faint,' Mary said, in a rather matter-of-fact voice.

'Well, don't,' Alice told her, still clinging to William's shoulders. 'Not now. Just get the door open, please.' The last word turned into another scream.

'Now what's the matter?' William wailed.

'It's down there, at your feet. I know it is. Oh, William . . .' and Alice's voice turned into a whimper of tears.

William stamped with his feet on the stone steps, trying to frighten away whatever was lurking there. Mary, realizing what he was doing, copied him. They both hopped up and down, banging their feet.

'It's all right for you, Alice,' Mary panted, 'William's holding you.' Then she felt William's hand gripping her arm.

'Listen,' he hissed in a strained whisper.

They all stopped moving and held their breath. Once

again they heard the strange dragging sound, only this time there seemed to be many more feet, so that it sounded like a soft stampede coming down towards them or a miniature avalanche, and mixed in amongst the awful pattering they could hear squeaks and hisses and whisperings.

'Oh,' Alice howled. 'There are hundreds of them.'

As she spoke the stairs behind them filled with glinting eyes and panting, squealing bodies. All that the three children could do was to huddle together, with their backs to the wooden door, and stare in horror at the wall of evil-smelling rats that pressed down upon them.

William felt something slide over his feet and at the same time Mary, standing just behind him, let out a gasp.

The wall of burning eyes pulled back and there was a sound like an excited sigh as a dark shape slithered up the stairs away from the feet of the children and then it stopped and turned, standing alone, to reveal itself as the rat they had seen in the secret room. It was a beast of such proportions that it made all the others seem small. It stood with its tail swishing and its sharp, pointed nose twitching then, very slowly, it opened its mouth in a hideous grin.

Alice clamped her hands over her eyes, which meant that she let go of her brother's shoulders. William almost toppled over, knocked off balance by this sudden movement, and he had to grope at the side wall of the stairs in order to steady himself. His hand brushed against an iron ring, set into the wall, and he held on to it to prevent himself falling. A moment later Mary, who was standing behind William and Alice and who was therefore slightly lower down the stairs, with her back pressed against the door, felt a sudden draught and the next thing she knew she was falling backwards as the door swung open. She just managed to regain her balance when William and Alice came toppling down behind her.

'Quick!' Mary screamed, breaking their fall, and she turned and raced down the steps, closely followed by the others. Soon they were at the foot of the spiral and out on the stone ledge at the side of the fireplace. Without any hesitation, Mary jumped for the ground and William and Alice followed immediately after her so that they all landed in a heap on the hearth of the great hall of Golden House.

'Ow!' William gasped, as Alice landed on his stomach.

'What happened?' she asked, trying to get up and digging an elbow into him.

'Alice!' he yelled. 'That's me when you've quite finished,' and pushing with all his strength he managed to roll her off him and to struggle up into a sitting position. One of his knees was smarting and covered with blood.

Mary was still lying where she had landed, but now she raised herself up and swung round to look back into the chimney. She saw William sitting just behind her inspecting his bleeding knee and Alice lying on the floor beside him. Then, just as she was about to speak to them, a rat jumped down from the side of the chimney on to the hearth.

'They're here,' she gasped, making William swing round in alarm, and the next moment the ground was covered with crawling, writhing, wriggling, grey, shining bodies. There were rats everywhere. There were rats on the floor and clinging to the walls. There were rats on the table and rats jumping on the chairs. It was as if the whole hall was awash with the creatures; tails swishing, teeth gnashing, feet scraping and all the time the terrible, over-excited, high-pitched squeaking.

'What's going on down there?' a voice called out from above them.

Looking up, Mary saw Jack leaning over the banister rail outside his bedroom door.

She only glanced up for a moment but in that short time all the rats disappeared. In fact, as Mary looked back again at her immediate surroundings she saw a grey-black shape slither under a gap in the wooden wainscot and, if she had not seen that, she could have been excused for thinking that she had dreamed the whole horrible episode.

'They've gone,' she whispered.

'William? Is that you?' Uncle Jack called.

William rose unsteadily on to his feet and moved towards the stairs.

'Yes,' he replied in a shaky voice.

'Who's that with you? Is it Alice?'

'And Mary,' Alice called out, sounding guilty. 'We're all here.'

'Look at you all,' Uncle Jack said, coming down the stairs into the gloomy hall. 'What have you been up to? You're covered in soot.'

The three children looked at each other and saw that what he said was true. There were smudges of black on their faces and hands.

'I've already prepared the fire,' Jack said, assuming that that was what they'd been doing. 'What time is it, anyway?' he asked, peering at his wrist watch in the half light. 'Eight o'clock. Oh, I meant to be up hours ago. Sorry, I must have overslept. We didn't have a very good night. Phoebe's in a lot of discomfort. I don't suppose any of you know if she should be, do you?'

The three children shook their heads and remained silent. They were still too shaken themselves to worry about Phoebe's welfare.

Uncle Jack stretched and shivered. He was only wearing a dressing gown. Which meant, Alice decided, that he probably slept with no pyjamas on, which was horribly rude.

'Come on then,' Jack said. 'Breakfast. I'll just put

some warmer clothes on . . .' Then he stopped in his tracks, halfway back up the stairs, and turned with a broad smile on his face. 'Oh, there!' he said. 'I nearly forgot what day it is! Happy Christmas, all of you!'

'Happy Christmas, Uncle Jack,' they replied, in unison, though they made it sound far from cheerful.

Jack looked at them thoughtfully for a moment.

'Whatever you were doing, forget about it now,' he told them. 'It's Christmas morning. Our first Christmas at Golden House. I want it to be a day we'll remember for the rest of our lives. Now go upstairs and wash and change and when you come down . . . I'll be ready.'

17

Thoughts and Feathers

'It was horrible,' Alice said, sitting on the side of her bed and shaking like a leaf.

'It wasn't nearly so bad for you,' Mary snapped at her. 'William was carrying you for most of the time. You didn't have them swarming all over your feet and up your legs, nibbling and clawing.'

'Oh, shut up, Mary. I can't stand it. You know how I hate rats.'

'Well, I hope you don't think I *like* them,' Mary told her. 'They were all slimy and slithery and their tails felt wet like worms . . .'

Alice screamed and dived under the eiderdown, shutting out the sound of her sister's voice.

Mary smiled a secret smile to herself. There was something very satisfying about frightening Alice. There always had been. It gave her quite a lot of pleasure, which sometimes she felt guilty about, but which didn't stop her doing it. Now, in order to round off her conquest, she tip-toed across the room and then jumped on top of her, squeaking and hissing like a mad person.

Alice let out a muffled yell and then they were rolling about on the bed, fighting, with the eiderdown between them.

William ran into the bedroom, holding a toothbrush and looking worried.

'Now what's happened?' he asked, looking round and half expecting the rats to have reappeared.

As he spoke, Mary, covered by the eiderdown, crashed down on to the floor with Alice kicking and yelling on top of her.

William leaned over and, grabbing Alice by the back of her sweater, he pulled her away with a hefty tug. Unfortunately Alice was still clinging to the eiderdown with a vice-like grip. There was a rending sound. William fell backwards on to the floor with Alice on top of him and a moment later the air was filled with swirling, flying goose feathers.

'Oh!' Alice said, opening her eyes. 'It's snowing indoors.'

'Oh, no!' William groaned. 'That's torn it!'

Mary emerged from a heap of white down that stirred and fluttered about her as she moved. She blinked and looked across at her brother and sister.

'Well,' she said, spitting feathers out of her mouth, 'it's certainly torn the eiderdown!'

'Oh, sausages!' Alice sighed, and then she started to giggle.

'Who's going to tell Phoebe?' William said in a grim voice and then he started giggling as well.

'You are, William,' Mary replied, scooping her hands in the feathers and making them fly and float in front of her, 'after all, you're the man!'

'Huh!' her brother responded. 'So much for women's lib!' and he lay back and hooted with laughter.

Alice was rolling on the floor, laughing so much that it made her stomach ache.

Mary looked at them both for a moment.

'William,' she hissed in a serious whisper, 'shut up for a minute. We don't have much time and we've masses to talk about.'

'Not rats, Mary, please,' Alice squealed. 'I don't want to talk about the rats,' and then she continued her giggling.

'But we must,' Mary insisted, getting up and crossing to the window. 'We can't just pretend it didn't happen.'

Behind her, William and Alice stopped laughing and lay on their backs, panting and silent, each of them remembering the events of the morning and trying to make some sense of what had happened.

Mary leaned on the window sill looking out at the steep rake of the roof and the white world beyond. The sky was heavy with clouds.

'It's like a black and white photograph,' she said to herself. And it was true; there was no colour and no movement outside, just the grey and white world of the snow, silent and untouched. 'As though we've slipped out of time into a sort of nowhere . . .'

'A limbo,' William told her, crossing to lean beside her and looking out at the half-lit, half-finished sketch of a view.

'Did we really meet a magician?' Alice said, in a small voice, from her position on the floor behind them.

'I suppose so,' William replied. 'What do you think, Mary?'

'Well, if we all think we saw the same things, we must have, mustn't we? There was an owl . . .'

'And the Magician had a silver walking stick,' Alice chimed in, 'with dragons on it.'

'And he was called Stephen Tyler,' William added, but he seemed to be talking more to himself. Then he frowned and dug his hands into his pockets, always an indication that he was thinking deeply.

'What, Will?' Mary asked, recognizing the signs.

'He said he built the steps up the chimney,' William said.

'But they're ever so old,' Alice protested.

'Maybe he meant the steps up the inside of the hearth. You know, the ones that get you on to the ledge at the bottom of the spiral staircase. 'Cause the actual stairs must belong to the tower of the old medieval building,' William continued, still working things out in his mind.

'Oh, well then they could have been done any time, couldn't they?' Alice said, sounding more cheerful.

But William shook his head.

'It's all in that book that Uncle Jack brought back from the town. Well, actually, it's on the sheets of paper that the librarian woman gave him.'

'What is?' Mary asked him.

'A list of all the people who lived here over the years. I can't remember it all. I didn't even read it all – because the beginning gave me such a shock that I felt creepy and wanted to get back to bed.'

'What, Will?' Mary was feeling creepy now.

'Gelden Place was some sort of religious house. Like an abbey or a . . . I don't know . . . what are those places religious people go to?'

'Churches?'

'Sort of, Alice, but . . . more like retreats, or something. Anyway – what happened in 1540?'

'King Henry the Eighth dissolved the monasteries,' Mary chimed in.

'Dissolved?' Alice exclaimed, trying to keep up with them.

'Got rid of them,' William told her, 'and Gelden Place was bought and made into a house for someone to live in.'

'Who by?' Mary asked, half knowing what the answer would be.

'That's the point,' William said, looking at her. 'According to the information that Uncle Jack brought, the property was purchased and restored as a private house in about 1550. And the person who bought it was Stephen Tyler.'

'But you asked him,' Mary exclaimed. 'He said he wasn't a descendant of that Stephen Tyler.'

'Exactly,' William replied.

'Well, then?' Mary insisted, as if that settled the matter.

'I think what he was saying was that he wasn't a *descendant* of Stephen Tyler – because he *is* that Stephen Tyler.'

There was a moment's silence in the room. Alice's eyes were round with sudden understanding.

'You mean he's the same man? Still alive now? But he must be hundreds of years old. How, William?' she gasped.

'I don't know. But that's what I think. And I'll tell you something else,' he said, his mind racing ahead, 'he said we would have to be tested, didn't he?'

'Yes, because we've got to help him.' Mary nodded, remembering.

'We're going to have to save all the worlds,' Alice groaned, making it sound like a pretty big job and exhausting.

'But what happened a moment after he told us that?' William asked, as the memories came flooding in.

The girls both frowned, going back into the events in their minds.

'The rat!' Alice said, suddenly.

'And it said we were going to be tested as well,' Mary exclaimed.

'Exactly.' William sounded triumphant. 'So, maybe the Magician turned himself into the rat to test us.'

'Ooooh!' Alice said triumphantly. 'How beastly of him. Frightening us all like that.'

'Well, at least we know that it was just a test and not the real thing,' William said, sounding relieved.

'I wonder if we passed the test,' Mary mused, and then she shivered. 'Have you finished in the bathroom, Will? I want to get ready and go down to the warm.'

'I've lost my toothbrush,' William said.

Alice found it for him, on the floor where he'd dropped it when he'd entered the fray between the girls. Suddenly the room was filled with activity as they all started to get ready for Christmas Day.

But if they hadn't been moving about and chattering so much, they might have heard the now familiar long, slow dragging sound of the rat's claws as it stealthily crawled away from its position behind the skirting board, where it had listened to every word that they'd been saying. And, if they had been able to follow it, they would have seen that it went through narrow tunnels and across rotten beams and up and down crumbling stone and plaster until it reached a part of the house that hadn't been occupied for many years. There the rat had its dwelling and there it made its secret plans. From that place it could hear all the sounds of the house and knew all the comings and goings of the people and creatures that lived in it. From there it had access to every corner of every room, for this was its kingdom and there wasn't anything that ever happened at Golden House that it didn't know about and that it didn't try to turn to its own best advantage.

For the rat was an evil creature and it served an evil master. But the children didn't know that yet.

18

Christmas at Golden House

The hall had been transformed when they came down. A great fire was blazing in the hearth, with flames so big that they licked right up the chimney into the darkness. The children ran towards it and looked anxiously up towards the ledge at the bottom of the staircase, but the draught up the chimney was such that all the smoke and flames were drawn away from the back corner and it looked as if it would be perfectly possible, if a little hot, to mount to the secret room even when a fire was alight.

'Very clever,' William whispered, admiring the scientific thinking behind the design. 'You see, the hot air rises, and the cold air, up in the chimney, draws on it. I expect the door halfway up the stairs is all part of it – it will stop the staircase becoming a sort of second chimney. Very clever indeed . . .'

'Oh, Mary, look!' Alice exclaimed. She had quickly become bored with William's lecture on the working of a chimney and had looked round at the rest of the hall.

In one corner, beside the front door, there was a

towering tree. It was so high that it almost touched the ceiling. It was covered with tiny pin-pricks of dancing light; candles so small that you could hardly see them. Each candle was held in a cup, clipped to the branches of the tree, and below each of these cups a silver star dangled and flashed, reflecting the light of the candles that surrounded it. The only other ornament was a huge golden star on the topmost branch. This star had a tail of golden chains that looped down over the lower branches until each individual glittering chain was lost to the sight in the lush, dark-green depths of the tree.

'It's beautiful,' Mary gasped.

The three children stood, with their backs to the fire, staring in wonder.

'But won't the candles burn out very quickly?' Alice said at last.

'They're night lights, I think,' William replied, taking a step towards the tree.

'Brilliant, boy!' Jack's voice said behind them. 'Go straight to the top of the form!' He was standing in the open kitchen doorway, through which wafted warm, delicious smells of cooking. In his arms he was carrying a huge bowl of holly, covered with red berries and with snow still nestling in some of the leaves. 'Where should I put this? Centre of the table?'

Jack placed the bowl on the table and then realized that the snow would drip on to the wood.

'I'd better let it melt first,' he said, speaking to himself. He placed the bowl on the stone floor, near to the tree.

'But – when did you do the tree, Uncle Jack?' Mary asked.

'Yesterday. It was hidden in one of the other rooms.'

'But how did you manage to get it in here?'

'Wheels!' Jack told her, with a laugh. 'It was a wonderful invention, the wheel! Look,' and he pointed at the barrel into which the base of the tree was fixed. The barrel was mounted on a square platform with little wheels, like a miniature cart.

'You made that?' William asked, impressed.

'No, actually. I found it in one of the outhouses. I am a firm believer in the ethic of retention! Never throw anything away – you never know when it might come in handy. Now, breakfast.' And as he spoke he marched across to the kitchen door followed by the others.

Phoebe was standing at the range, toasting bread on a long fork in front of the open grate. She looked round as they came into the room, leaning one hand on the back of her waist and holding the toasting-fork in front of her with the other. She looked tired and drawn and there were wisps of hair falling across her face. Her big, pregnant stomach bulged under a long, plain blue dress. But she smiled as she saw them and even Alice, who was determined not to be won over, had to admit later that she did seem to make an effort to be cheerful.

'There you are,' she cried. 'Breakfast first and then presents around the tree, how's that?' The smell of toast and coffee mingled with other cooking smells and with the scent of the wood smoke from the hall.

'Happy Christmas, everyone,' Phoebe added, and she slipped the toast off the fork and added it to the toast rack on the table.

As soon as breakfast was over the children ran back upstairs to get their own presents, which they added to the ones already piled up under the tree in the hall. Then, just as ten was being chimed by the grandfather clock, they all gathered in front of the fire and Jack appeared from the kitchen carrying a tray. On it was an ice bucket out of which a bottle of champagne poked and a group of glasses.

'Champagne,' he announced dramatically, as he entered.

With a pop and a lot of fizzing the cork came off and Jack poured the frothing liquid into five glasses. Then he handed a glass to each of them. Phoebe was sitting in one of the wooden armchairs in front of the fire and the children were kneeling on the hearth rug.

'Don't drink until we've had the toast,' he warned them.

Alice didn't want any more toast and said so, which the others seemed to think was a huge joke and so she let them think how clever she'd been without really being quite sure what they were laughing at. Then Jack raised his glass.

'We've got lots of things to drink to: our first Christmas here at Golden House, the fact that we're all together, the forthcoming baby. But I think we'll only drink to one thing, shall we?'

'Oh, hurry up, please, Uncle Jack,' Mary cried. 'I can't wait to taste the champagne.'

'All right then,' he laughed and he held the glass out in front of him. 'To your parents, kids; wherever they are and whatever they're doing.'

'To William and Mary and Alice's parents,' Phoebe said, raising her glass.

'To Mummy and Daddy,' William said, feeling a lump forming in his throat.

Alice glanced uncomfortably at Mary, uncertain what was expected of her. She saw Mary raise her glass. There were tears in her eyes.

'Mummy and Dad,' she mumbled.

'Oh stop it, all of you,' Alice cried out, unable to stop tears spilling out of her eyes and splashing down her cheeks. She took a huge gulp of the champagne and a moment later sneezed violently.

Jack threw back his head and laughed.

'That'll be the bubbles!' he said. 'Right now – there's orange juice here if you'd rather have it?'

'Yes please, Uncle Jack,' Mary said at once. 'Tell the

truth, I'm not very keen on champagne.'

'Shame on you, child! One day you'll think it's the finest drink in the world.'

'Can I have orange juice as well, please?' William asked, setting down his glass of champagne with only a sip taken out of it.

'Can I have yours, Will?' Alice asked, reaching for it.

'No, Jack. It's too strong,' Phoebe told him.

'Sorry, love,' Jack said, retrieving the full glass and also Mary's glass and putting them back on the tray. 'One glass is the limit then it's on to the orange juice.'

'But what'll you do with their glasses?' Alice pleaded. 'You'll surely not throw it away.'

'I most certainly will not,' he told her and he gave her a grin and a wink. 'Now, presents!' he said, crossing to the tree.

The children had bought a box of chocolates for Phoebe and Jack. Mary got a pencil sharpener shaped like a whale from William, and a poster of Alice's favourite pop star from Alice. Actually Mary didn't like him much, but Alice said she was crazy and that she'd have the poster in her bedroom, if Mary didn't want it. William got a puzzle from Mary; it was a little square box, filled with minute ball bearings that had to be fitted into a heart shape. He got a different poster of the same star from Alice. William couldn't stand him either. Alice got a puzzle from Mary – a similar square box to William's, but in hers the ball bearings had to fit into a star – and she got a pencil sharpener from William in the shape of an elephant, which she considered horribly rude, because the pencil to be sharpened had to be stuck into the elephant's bottom. They all got money from their mother and father and a special letter each, which they read quickly and then put in their pockets to be enjoyed in privacy later.

But the presents from Jack and Phoebe were the real surprises. Phoebe had knitted each of them jumpers in the most beautiful rich, jewel colours. William's was black, red and white, in a sort of random geometric pattern. Mary's was pale misty blue and pinks with stronger greens and looked a bit like a picture of a hazy summer morning in the countryside. Alice's was all bright oranges and yellows and blues, like a sunburst. They were all big and comfortable, with loose round necks and long sleeves.

Phoebe had also knitted Jack a jumper. His was dark green and dark blue and had a spiky sun in burnt orange-red on the front.

'And finally,' Jack said, picking up the last parcel and reading the label, 'this one is for Miss Taylor, with endless love from me!'

'Liz Taylor?' Mary said, surprised. 'The film star?'

'No, chump,' Jack said, with a laugh. 'Miss Taylor the most beautiful mother-to-be in all the world.'

'Jack!' Phoebe protested, taking the parcel and blushing. She tore off the paper carefully. Phoebe was obviously one of those people who used wrapping paper again. Inside was a long flat black box. This she opened and then the children heard her gasp.

'Oh, Jack,' she exclaimed, 'wherever did you find it?'

The children crowded round to see what it was she had been given.

Lying on the dark velvet interior of the box was a pendant on a thin gold chain. The pendant design was a silver moon and a golden sun held in an oval frame of a dark, red metal.

'It's beautiful,' she said.

'Don't you recognize it?' he asked her.

Phoebe looked at it closely and frowned.

'Is it the one you found? But that was black and rusty.'

'The very same. I'm not sure if I can really claim it's a present from me. It's from the house more like. I found it in the hearth here,' he continued, turning to look at the children, 'soon after we moved in. It was just lying on the hearthstone. But the funny thing was, I'd brushed the hearth down not half an hour before and it hadn't been there then. Goodness knows where it came from. It was all black and horrible – you could scarcely make out the design even. I didn't give it much thought. I just took it upstairs to our room and put it in a drawer for safe keeping. Then, one day about a month ago, I came across it again and I thought I'd just see what it looked like cleaned up . . .'

'It's beautiful, Uncle Jack,' Mary told him, still looking at the pendant.

'I'm pretty sure it's pure silver and pure gold,' Jack said, looking over Mary's shoulder, 'though I've no idea what the red metal is. Aren't you going to put it on?' he asked, turning to Phoebe. 'I had the chain made in the town.'

Phoebe lifted her long hair and slipped the chain round her neck. Then with both hands behind her head she fiddled with the catch.

'Let me, Phoebe?' Mary said.

'Thanks. Would you?' Phoebe asked her, sounding almost shy.

Mary fitted the little ring into the catch and settled the chain on Phoebe's neck, then they all stood back to admire the pendant. The chain Jack had bought was quite short, so that the pendant rested on the smooth skin above the scoop of the neckline of her dark blue dress. She pressed her hand against it, her cheeks colouring again.

'I shall treasure it for ever,' she said quietly and Jack leaned over and kissed her tenderly.

'Happy Christmas,' he whispered to her and then he turned and smiled at the children. 'Happy Christmas, everyone.'

Later the children went out for a walk. The sky was so dark and overcast that it was as though night was approaching, although it was only the middle of the morning.

'Where d'you think the pendant came from?' Mary asked as they crunched through the snow, keeping to the confines of the drive where it was less deep and where the ground was at least level.

'Could it have fallen down from the secret room?' Alice wondered. 'It's the sort of pattern the magician would have made, isn't it?'

'Yes,' William agreed. 'But it couldn't have fallen from the room; not down all those stairs and, if it had, it wouldn't have landed plonk in the middle of the hearth.'

'Maybe there's treasure up the actual chimney,' Mary suggested.

'Oh, I don't want to have to climb up there as well,' Alice wailed.

'Maybe the Magician gave it,' William said.

'But – why would he?' Mary asked.

William shrugged.

'I don't know. I don't know anything. There are too many strange things happening.' He sounded quite depressed about it. William was one of those people who like to be in control; who don't like having to admit the unknown or the unexplainable. He trudged along, dragging his feet in the snow, his hands plunged into his pockets, his forehead creased with a frown.

'What do vegetables have for Christmas dinner?' Alice asked, oblivious to her brother's mood.

'Vegetarians,' Mary corrected her wearily, as though she'd had to do so innumerable times before.

'Oh, what does it matter if I don't use the right word? You know what I mean. I know what I mean. What does it matter?' Alice protested crossly.

They walked on in silence, each of them lost in their own thoughts.

Eventually William looked at his watch.

'Midday,' he announced. 'We'd better turn back. Phoebe said lunch would be at one.'

'I'm starving,' Alice wailed.

'You're always starving, Alice,' Mary muttered.

''Cause I'm growing. I need fuel for my growth. Turkey with little sausages and roast potatoes and stuffing and bacon and more sausages and gravy . . .'

'Carrots and parsnips and cabbage and sprouts,' William chanted. 'Turnips and swedes and . . .'

'Artichokes!' Mary cut in, triumphantly. 'Jerusalem artichokes!'

'What are they?' Alice squealed, prepared for the worst.

'You remember, Alice,' William said, sounding sinister.

'The nobbly grey things that Mother used sometimes to make into a soup,' Mary told her, grinning maliciously.

'Nobbly grey things?' Alice asked, appalled.

'The soup that made us poop!' William announced, beginning to laugh.

'Oh, William,' Alice cried, remembering. 'You mean those horrible potato things that made us pop all night?'

'All night?' Mary said, hooting with laughter.

'You farted for a week at least, Ally!' William said, shaking with laughter.

'You'll have to put money in the swear box for that,' Alice shouted.

'We haven't got one,' Mary cried.

'I didn't swear,' William told her.

'You did, William Constant. You said farted.'

'Oooh! Rude, Alice, rude!' Mary said, pointing at her sister. 'You said farted!'

'So did you, then,' Alice replied, beginning to laugh as well.

'We all said it,' William announced. 'So, let's all say it again.'

In unison they shouted the word so that it echoed back and forth across the steep, snow-filled valley.

'Farted. Farted . . . farted . . . farted.'

They arrived at the front door shaking with laughter.

Jack was standing in the porch, a worried look on his face.

'Oh, there you are,' he said. 'I've been looking for you. Come in, quick.'

'What's the matter, Uncle Jack?' William said, as they kicked off their wellington boots.

'It's Phoebe,' Jack answered, grimly.

'Is she ill again?' Mary asked, unwinding her scarf.

'I think . . .' Jack hesitated for a moment and then continued, 'I think she's started.'

'Started?' Alice asked, confused as usual.

'The baby,' Jack told her. 'The baby is on its way.'

19

A Journey Through the Blizzard

Phoebe was leaning against the sink in the kitchen. Jack crossed quickly to her, putting an arm round her, supporting her.

'How is it now?' he asked quietly.

'The same,' she replied, brushing his cheek gently with the back of her hand. 'Don't worry, I'll be all right. Women've been having babies since Adam and Eve.'

The children stood by the kitchen door, feeling awkward. It was as though they were eavesdropping on a private conversation. But Phoebe looked over her shoulder and smiled at them, making them feel included in the scene.

'I'm sorry,' she said, 'this is really ruining Christmas!'

'You can't help it,' William told her, feeling suddenly protective towards her. 'It isn't your fault and, besides, the birth of the baby is much more important. We can have Christmas any day.'

Mary looked at her brother with pride. What nice things he said sometimes. But Alice still believed Phoebe to be a witch and so she wasn't so generous. In her heart of hearts she thought it a bit typical, Phoebe making yet another fuss, when they should all be sitting down to vegeburgers or whatever other horrible stuff she'd prepared for them. But she didn't say anything, because Phoebe did look sorry and besides Uncle Jack was so obviously worried.

Then Phoebe put both her hands on the back of her waist and straightened her back, crying out as though in pain.

Jack held her to him, looking desperate. Then, when the spasm had passed, he guided her towards a chair by the kitchen range.

'You sit there while I get the Land-Rover ready.'

'Are we going?' she asked.

'The sooner I get you into the town hospital the better. Alice, can you get a blanket from our bedroom please? And Mary, if you go with her, you'll find a suitcase already packed by the wardrobe. Bring it down and then get a couple of hot-water bottles from the bottom of that dresser and' – as he spoke he swung the kettle over the flames of the fire – 'keep an eye on this, will you? It'll soon boil. But don't fill the bottles. I'll do that when I come back. William, you come with me. I may need help starting the Land-Rover.' Jack strode towards the back door, still speaking as he went. 'Get your wellingtons from the front porch and meet me round in the yard.'

Then he was gone and the door closed with a bang, shutting out the cold air.

Mary and Alice hurried out of the room to do their jobs and William raced after them into the hall, leaving Phoebe sitting awkwardly in the chair, staring into the flames of the fire.

'Will she be all right d'you think, Will?' Mary called, as she raced up the stairs with Alice just behind her.

'I don't know, do I?' William snapped, crossly. 'I've never been with anyone when they're having a baby before.'

It was another of those out-of-his-control situations that he hated so much. He hurried to the front door and out into the porch, where he pulled on his boots.

As he ran through the deep snow round to the back yard, he noticed a black and white dog crouching on the ground at a distance, its tail beating slowly backwards and forwards in the air, watching the house. But before he had time really to take this in he was faced by an altogether different surprise.

Jack was standing beside the Land-Rover where it was parked under the roof of a lean-to barn. He was staring in disbelief at the wheels of the vehicle.

'What's the matter, Uncle Jack?' William asked, hurrying towards him and sensing that something bad had happened.

Jack shook his head, but didn't look at William.

'I can't believe it,' he said. 'I've never seen anything like this before.'

'What?' William asked, reaching his side. Then he saw for himself and didn't need his uncle to tell him.

Every one of the four tyres of the shooting brake was ripped and torn and lying in shreds on the ground. The metal of the wheels dug into the packed earth.

'It's unusable of course,' Jack said, more to himself. 'But how could it have happened?'

He turned and scanned the flat snowy expanse of the yard, as if hoping for some answering clue to be lying around. And in a way there was one and it was William who found it: a track like two narrow sledge marks that led from the wall of the house to the barn and from the barn back to the house.

'Some animal, d'you suppose?' William asked.

Jack bent down and examined the marks.

'Rat,' he replied.

The one word sent a shiver through William.

'But what would it want with rubber tyres? Oh, damn. Phoebe told me she could hear a rat, but I didn't pay any attention to her. Now what am I going to do? I can't drive her to the hospital.' He looked up at the dark, threatening clouds. 'The snow will come soon, then we won't be able to get in or out of the valley.'

'Isn't there a telephone box near?' William asked, desperately trying to think of some way to help.

'Yes, there's one down on the moor road, just before the turning into this valley.'

'How far would that be?'

'About two miles, I think. But what good will it be – if the snow comes? I need to get Phoebe to a hospital. And the sooner the better, by the look of that sky.' As he spoke they both looked up at the dark, lowering clouds. They looked as if they were ready to burst under the weight of the threatening snow. 'If I leave it much longer, then nothing will be able to get in or out of the valley.'

'They could send a helicopter, Uncle Jack. You often see that on television news.'

'You're right, William. I must go at once,' Jack said, striding towards the kitchen door.

'I'll come as well,' William called, hurrying after him.

'You'd be better off staying here,' Jack told him.

'No,' William answered, emphatically. 'Anything could happen. We don't know how much the snow has drifted or if the road is passable. At least with two of us there'd be more chance of getting through.'

Jack looked at his nephew for a moment, and then he nodded.

They went into the kitchen together and Jack explained to Phoebe what had happened.

'No, Jack,' she protested. 'We'll be able to manage somehow.'

'I'm not taking any further risks,' Jack replied, almost crossly. 'We should have been much more prepared for this.'

'It's my fault,' Phoebe said, in a forlorn voice. 'I wanted to have the baby here at Golden House. I should have listened to you.'

'No time for remorse now, love,' Jack said, giving her a hug. 'You just concentrate on holding on till help arrives. William, put really warm clothes on. And you girls, keep the fires burning in the hall and here in the kitchen. We'll be back as soon as we can.'

The warmest sweater that William had got was the one Phoebe had knitted for him. He wore it with his school scarf and his anorak on top. Thick socks filled out his wellington boots, into which he tucked his trousers, and a pair of gloves completed the outfit.

He and Jack, similarly protected against the biting wind, set off as soon as they were ready, crunching over the crisp ground. Alice and Mary stood in the porch watching them go.

'There's my dog,' Alice said, pointing, and then the girls watched the animal as it bounded across the snow towards William and Jack. There it stopped and they saw William pointing back towards the house.

'I wonder what he's saying,' Alice mused. 'He's my dog.'

'Go back,' William was telling the dog. 'Look after the girls.'

The dog whined and pawed the ground.

'Do as you're told,' William said in a stern voice. Then he added, 'Please.'

The dog leaped up in the air, doing a somersault and barking gleefully, then it turned tail and streaked back across the white expanse of lawn towards the front door.

'Friend of yours?' Jack enquired, watching the animal.

'Yes, I think so,' William replied. Then he raised a hand and waved to his sisters, framed in the porch, and watched as Alice knelt to welcome the dog into her arms. 'Well, really, he's more a friend of Alice's,' he added.

'Come on then,' Jack said, looking grimly at the clouds. 'Let's get a move on.' As he spoke the first big blobs of snow floated out of the sky.

The first part of the journey wasn't too hard. Although the snow was falling heavily and made visibility difficult, the house lay in a hollow and was protected from the north. But when they turned out of the gates and struck out over the first hill they could feel the wind building up and when they reached the brow they met it full in their faces.

Here the snow was being driven at a sharp angle and it stung at their exposed skin like needles. William put up his hands to protect his eyes and peered into the swirling heart of the blizzard. The trees on either side of them bent under the fury of the gale and great piles of drifted snow blocked their way.

Uncle Jack shouted something, but his words were snatched away from them by the howling storm and William missed them completely.

Jack beckoned and held out a hand, which William grabbed hold of. Together they fought their way to the side of the track and crouched down behind a wall, which gave them some shelter.

'We'll never make it,' Jack gasped.

'We must!' William told him.

'But even a helicopter couldn't get through this storm,' Jack shouted against the roar of the wind.

'It can't last for ever,' William insisted. 'If we get to the telephone box we can at least put up the alarm. They'll get through when they can. It's better than doing nothing.'

Jack looked round them, nodding.

'We'd be better off up in the trees,' he said. 'There's less wind there and less snow on the ground.'

William surveyed the steep side of the valley doubtfully.

'Is there a path up there?' he asked.

'I don't know,' Jack admitted, 'but it's our only hope. The snow's drifting on the track. We'll never get through that way. Come on.' He held out a hand and pulled William up on to his feet. 'You're the one who said we must at least try.'

Jack led the way across the narrow, rising field with the wind tearing at them so that they had to lean against it. Then they reached the tree line. The branches were clattering and snapping in the gale but at least there was less snow and, although it was dark and gloomy in the interior of the wood, it was easier to see without the snow driving into their faces. The ground here was very steep, however, and this made them move slowly.

'If only we could find some sort of a path,' Jack muttered.

As he spoke, William saw something red flashing amongst the trees, higher up the bank, and a moment later the fox broke cover, staring down at them, its breath smoking on the frosty air.

'The fox,' William cried, excitedly.

'Where?' Jack asked, but before he could catch a glimpse of it, it had turned and disappeared once more in amongst the trees.

William frowned. He felt certain that in some way the fox was communicating with him. But what was it that he was saying?

'What is it that you want?' a voice that he half recognized whispered inside his head.

'A path,' William whispered back and, as the thought occurred to him, so he realized that the fox was showing him the way.

'Come on, Uncle Jack,' he said, excitedly. 'There'll be a path higher up.' And as he spoke he started to scramble up the steep bank in the direction that the fox had gone.

It wasn't much of a path, just a narrow indentation

that wound its way through the tall fir trees along the side of the hill, but it certainly made the going easier for Jack and William. They found they were able to get up quite a speed and were almost running across the uneven ground. The light inside the wood was no more than a faint glimmer and the sound of the storm was cut off by the vast trees that towered above them. For the second time William felt he was in a strange limbo world, between two points and not belonging to either of them. He searched in the gloom for any sign of the fox but it seemed to have disappeared. He was sorry. He knew now that the fox was his friend. After all, the Magician had said it was a friend of his and the Magician wanted them to help him. So any friend of the Magician's was no doubt also a friend of theirs. This sudden memory of the Magician made him stop in his tracks. Supposing, just supposing, he thought, that this terrible time they were having – with Phoebe about to deliver her baby and the storm raging and the rat ruining the tyres of the brake . . . just supposing that all these events were part of the Magician's test. For that was what he'd said:

'You must be tested . . . to see if you're worthy of the name Constant . . .' or words something like that.

'It must be a pretty big job he needs us for,' William concluded.

But then all further thought was abruptly curtailed

for, ahead of him along the track, he saw Jack pitch forward and fall awkwardly to the ground. A moment later William also narrowly avoided tripping on the thick root of a tree that straddled the path and had caused the accident.

'Uncle Jack,' he called, dodging the root and running to where Jack was lying, breathing heavily, face down on the ground. 'Are you all right?' he asked, kneeling beside him and trying to lift his shoulders.

'Not very,' Jack groaned. 'Well, let's say I've been better.' Then he let out a cry of pain.

'Where does it hurt?' William asked.

'The leg,' Jack replied grimly. As he spoke he managed to haul himself into a sitting position. He felt with his hands down below the knee. 'Bother,' he said. 'I think I've broken it. Of all the stupid . . . I can't move, William. But I must . . . see if you can find me a stick . . .' Then he let out another bellow of agony.

'You can't, Uncle Jack. You're in too much pain.'

'Well, I can't stop here, can I?'

'Let me go on alone,' William said. 'If I can get to the phone box, I'll let the police know what's happened and then I'll come back for you.'

'You'll never make it on your own,' Jack groaned.

'Yes, I will,' William told him in a determined voice. 'If I must, I will.'

He scrambled to his feet and started to run along the

path, leaving Jack lying back, propped against the trunk of a tree.

William heard the heavy breathing first; a panting sound. He glanced to his right and thought he saw the red shape of the fox, running beside him, in amongst the trees. But then, a moment later, he realized that the panting was coming from his open mouth and that his tongue was hanging out. Looking down he saw a red paw hitting the earth beneath him and then another one came into view. He looked back over his shoulder and saw the full length of his sleek red body, with the bushy tail streaming in the breeze caused by the speed of his chase. He put his nose down to the ground, sniffing the earth. He could smell rabbit and badger and then the strong odour of deer. He looked up, pricking his ears, his nose twitching in the keen air.

He swung left, off the path and chased down the nearly sheer side of the hill, weaving in and out of the tall trunks of the trees. The smell of the snow was stronger now and so was the sound of the blizzard.

Then a moment later he broke the cover of the trees and stood, brilliant red and panting, in the swirling grey and white world of the storm.

He was standing on the steep side of the hill. Far below, across several fields, he could see the red roof of the telephone box.

He lifted his head, stretching his neck so that he could

feel the muscles pulling on the shoulders of his front legs, then, filling his lungs with the icy wind, he barked at the wind.

What a surprising noise, William thought. So sharp and loud.

Then he plunged down the hill, his feet scarcely touching the surface of the snow. Ahead a grey stone wall barred the way. William gathered his strength and sprang, using the muscles of his back legs, and cleared the wall without hesitation. Three times he jumped the walls. It was as near to flying as he'd ever experienced.

Then, as suddenly, William was standing outside the telephone box, in the raging storm, and the fox was panting and stretching at a distance from him, in the shelter of a mound of bushes.

Without pausing to consider the strange and magical event that had just taken place, William forced open the kiosk door and reached for the telephone.

Taking off his gloves he rubbed his hands to restore the circulation, then he inserted his finger in the old-fashioned dial and spun out three nines.

'Emergency?' a voice spoke in his ear. 'Which service do you require?'

20
Spot

Mary stood watching William and Jack disappear into the gloomy distance. She felt suddenly depressed. William always got all the adventures.

Alice was kneeling at her feet, making a fuss of the dog.

'Oh, Mary, he's gorgeous,' she cried, looking up. 'Do stroke him if you want to.'

She was behaving, Mary thought, as if she owned the animal already. And, to be fair, the dog seemed to have decided that Alice was going to be his friend for life. He sat in front of her, his tail wagging on the stones of the porch, gazing at her with obvious adoration.

'What shall we call him?' Alice said, holding his head in both her hands and letting him give her face a good wash with his tongue.

'I don't know how you can let him do that,' Mary said with a shudder. 'Dogs eat all sorts of muck and horrible things.'

'I don't care,' Alice replied huffily. 'I shall call you "Spot", until I think of a better name, because of the white bit on your face,' she told her new friend.

'Oh, Alice!' Mary exclaimed. 'That's not very original! "Spot"? There must be hundreds of dogs called "Spot"! Besides, he's probably already got a name – and an owner.'

Alice looked crestfallen.

'D'you think so?' she asked sadly. 'Well, whoever it is shouldn't let him wander about in the cold. Can we take him inside?'

'Please yourself,' Mary said, turning away from her and going back into the hall. 'He's got nothing to do with me. He isn't my dog.'

She felt cross with herself for being so grumpy, but she couldn't help it. Sometimes these moods came over her and there was nothing she could do about them. When they did, she hated everybody including herself and really all she wanted to do was to crawl into a corner where no one could see her and cry.

The fire was burning low in the hearth.

Mary crossed to the pile of logs that were stacked at one side of the chimney and picked one up. It was terribly heavy, and she had to use both hands to move it. She crossed to the burning mound and dropped it into the embers. At once little flames licked round the edges of it. She put a few more logs on, forming them into a sort of wigwam round the glowing centre, then she knelt on the hearth rug watching the flames growing in strength and the fire leaping once more into life.

The front door was still open and out on the porch Alice was talking quietly to Spot.

'Stay there,' she was telling him. 'I'll come back in a minute. Stay!'

She rose and backed towards the door. The dog remained stationary, watching her, his tail wagging.

'Oh, Mary, look,' Alice murmured. 'He's ever so well behaved.' Then she turned and ran through the hall to the kitchen.

Phoebe was bending over the range oven when Alice entered.

'Phoebe,' she called excitedly, 'can the dog come in? Please. He's very well behaved and he's called Spot and it's horribly cold out there and he won't be any trouble . . .'

During this gabble of words Phoebe carried a large oval dish to the table and uncovered it. Steam rose all around her face and the most delicious smell wafted in Alice's direction.

'Oooh,' Alice said, stopping in full flood, 'what is it?'

'Just a lot of old vegetables and things,' Phoebe said with a smile. Then she straightened her back, gripping the side of the table, and her face clouded with pain.

'Are you all right?' Alice asked. Then, when Phoebe didn't answer her, she backed into the hall, calling:

'Mare, can you come?'

'Mary was deep in gloom on the hearth rug and hardly seemed to hear her.

'Mary!' Alice called, louder. 'I think Phoebe can't hold on.'

'What?' Mary said, cross that she was being disturbed. 'What are you talking about, Alice?'

'Something's wrong with Phoebe,' she gasped, still standing in the doorway, staring into the kitchen.

Mary rose quickly and hurried towards her.

'Are you all right, Phoebe?' she asked.

Phoebe half turned towards her, lifting a hand from the table almost as though she was waving, then in slow motion she began to topple backwards.

'Phoebe!' Mary cried, dashing towards her. 'Alice, quick, she's going to fall.'

The two girls lunged at Phoebe and grabbed her arms, holding her upright.

'Where should we take you?' Mary asked.

'The hall,' Phoebe whispered. 'Just help me to the fire, please.'

With great care they helped her out of the kitchen and across the hall to the rug in front of the fire. There they lowered her gently and, with Spot nuzzling up to her, and licking her hand, she settled herself on the ground.

'Shouldn't you go to bed?' Mary asked her, uncertainly.

Spot, who was sitting beside her, looked over his shoulder at the long flight of stairs.

'No,' Phoebe told her, 'Spot's right. It's a long way. I'll be better here, in front of the fire. The bedroom is cold and . . . should anything happen, it'll be easier here.'

'What might happen?' Mary said, dreading the answer.

'Well with any luck, I might have a baby!' Phoebe answered, with a gentle laugh. 'Will you help me, Mary?'

Mary swallowed and felt her cheeks burning.

'I wouldn't know what to do,' she said, brushing her hair away from her eyes with a nervous gesture.

'I think we'll work it out between us,' Phoebe told her, then she looked at the front door, which was still ajar, letting in volumes of ice-cold air. 'I suppose Jack and William will be far gone by now?' she said.

Alice got up and crossed over to the front door, looking out.

'I can't see them,' she said. 'And it's starting to snow.'

'D'you want us to get them?' Mary asked, eagerly. Somehow she thought she'd much rather go out into the storm than have to help deliver a baby.

'No,' Phoebe replied, tension in her voice. 'I think I'll need you here.'

'Oh, help!' Alice whispered. 'Does this mean you're not going to be able to hold on, Phoebe?'

'I'll try,' Phoebe said with a half-hearted smile. 'Close the door, Alice. It's cold with it open.'

'Shall we get you some bedding?' Mary was suddenly inspired. 'Blankets and pillows?'

'Yes, that would be a good idea,' Phoebe said, gratefully.

'I don't think we could manage a mattress.'

'No, just some pillows. And some blankets and the eiderdown.'

'What about hot-water bottles?' Alice suggested.

'Please. But get the bedding first. And Mary,' she called, as the two girls were hurring away up the stairs. 'Bring my nightgown. You'll have to help me undress.'

'All right,' Mary said and she and Alice clattered up the stairs to the gallery.

As they turned towards Phoebe's bedroom door, the grey shape of the rat slipped away from its vantage place by the banister.

'Did you see?' Alice whispered, as they went into the bedroom.

Mary nodded.

'It's all right, Ally,' she said. 'If the rat is really the Magician in disguise, then he's probably here to help us.'

But Alice looked doubtful. She couldn't quite bring herself to believe in a helpful rat.

They made Phoebe as comfortable as possible in front of the fire. The pains that she kept getting were coming more frequently and Mary suspected that this was a sign that the birth was getting closer. But Phoebe tried to reassure them. She told them to get some soup but said that she didn't want any herself. She also suggested they should have hot water ready.

'To wash the baby,' she explained. 'And we'll need lots of towels. I expect I'll sweat quite a bit. Having a baby is strenuous exercise!'

Alice and Mary sat on the rug beside her, eating steaming soup, and Spot crouched on the other side of her eating a bowl of cereal, soaked in a little warm soup.

'We'll have to get proper food for him,' Phoebe said.

Poor Spot, Alice thought. He'll have to be a vegetable as well. But she didn't say anything, because she didn't want to upset Phoebe.

Every so often Spot would look up, listening and sniffing the air. Once or twice this was accompanied by a long, low growl.

'What is it?' Alice would ask him and he'd sit up on his hind legs, looking up at the gallery above.

'He can hear something or sense something,' Phoebe said in a weak voice on one occasion. Then she also held up her head, listening intently.

The sound of the rat's claws as it scraped along the gallery were distinctly audible.

'The rat,' Phoebe said, with fear in her eyes.

Spot sat up, barking. Then he padded towards the bottom of the stairs, where he stood looking up, listening intently and growling.

'No. No, it's all right, Spot,' Mary said, running over to him. 'The rat's a friend,' she whispered in his ear. 'He's the Magician.'

But Spot continued to growl deeply and although he licked her hand he wouldn't return to the fire but remained at the foot of the stairs, staring up at the landing. All the hairs on his back were bristling, as his eyes probed the dark and his nose sniffed out possible danger.

As the afternoon wore on the wind outside grew in volume until it howled and moaned around the house. The light in the hall was dim, but the fire burned brightly and luckily Jack had got in a whole load of logs so the girls were able to replenish it whenever it was needed.

Phoebe fell into a feverish sleep. She was sweating profusely, but at the same time she felt quite cold. Mary bathed her brow with clean water from time to time and Alice held her hand.

'I don't think she is a witch,' she told Mary. 'Or if she is, then she's a good one – like the little round blonde one in *The Wizard of Oz*. But I still don't understand why they didn't get married first. I mean, what will the baby be called? It should have its father's name. But she isn't his wife so what name will the baby have? His or hers?'

'It doesn't matter now, Ally,' Mary told her. 'Not at the moment. Whatever name it has is only something we give it – like you called Spot, Spot. But that's just us. Spot was a dog before you ever called him Spot and the baby will be a baby in the same way.'

'I think marriage would be hypocritical for me,' Phoebe interrupted her, speaking with her eyes closed and sounding almost as if she was speaking to herself. 'I don't go to church and I certainly don't need a piece of legal paper to prove that Jack and I belong together. What would be the point of that? We know we belong together. We love each other. That's enough, surely?'

'But . . .' Alice couldn't stop herself protesting.

'What, Alice? Does it shock you? Is that it?' Phoebe asked her, opening her eyes and looking directly at her. 'How very old-fashioned of you! Can't you see how happy Jack and I are together? What more do you want?'

'But the baby, Phoebe,' Alice insisted, 'it won't have a proper name.'

'I thought you came from a sensible family, Alice. Of course it'll have a name. My name. Taylor.'

'Taylor?' Mary said, in a puzzled voice.

'But what if it wants to have Uncle Jack's name? What then?' Alice challenged her. 'Green's a jolly good name, you know. Mum was a Green once.'

'Then it can take Jack's name. For goodness' sake! Don't make so many problems. It can have Jack's name, or my name, or both our names with a hyphen. It isn't important, Alice. What's important is that the baby comes to know who she or he really is. You're not just Alice Constant . . .'

'I am. Of course I am.'

'No, you're much more than that. You are a person in your own right.'

'I'm Alice Constant,' Alice insisted.

'Well,' Phoebe replied, wearily. 'The baby can decide which name it wants. It can either be a Green or a Taylor . . .'

'Taylor,' Mary said again, thoughtfully. Then she clapped her hands. 'Of course,' she cried, 'I bet once your family used to be called Tyler.'

But neither of the others was listening to her. Phoebe had fallen once more into a troubled sleep and Alice was kneeling beside Spot, trying to calm him. He was pacing up and down, growling and barking and pawing the stairs impatiently.

'It's all right, Spot,' she told him. 'I hate rats as well. But honestly, we think this one is the Magician. So he's probably a friend. You see, we're being tested . . . oh, it all gets very confusing and I can't follow some of it . . .'

'The Magician isn't the rat,' Spot's voice growled in Alice's head. It gave her such a surprise that she stopped speaking.

'All right then,' the voice growled again – but only in her thoughts. She couldn't hear anything exactly; she could just think-hear. 'All right. Come with me. We'll soon find out if the rat is the Magician's friend.'

'Oh,' said Alice in her mind. 'I'm not sure about that. Rats scare me a lot.' But as she spoke, she lifted her nose, sniffing the air.

The scent of rat was strong. A horrible smell; the smell of fear and the gutter and decaying things. Alice pricked her ears, listening. The rat wasn't moving; but she could hear it breathing and its heart beating.

Quietly, Alice rose from the floor on to her four legs. Her tail was down; the hair on her back crackled with electricity. She stood, poised at the bottom of the stairs. Then slowly, step by step, she climbed up to the gallery.

The stench of the rat grew stronger. But she wasn't frightened by it. She felt only distaste and a deep anger. Reaching the landing she paused and looked down into the hall. Mary was bathing Phoebe's brow again and seemed oblivious to what was going on. The firelight glowed in the half light and the figures on the hearth rug looked as if they were part of a picture; one of those old oil paintings, dark and shiny with age, with what little colour there was all in the centre and the edges faded and mysterious.

'Right,' Spot's voice growled in her head, 'any friend of the Magician's is a friend of ours,' and she looked stealthily round the newel post and along the uneven floor of the gallery.

The rat was well hidden on a jutting stone that stuck out from the side wall of the hall and was one of the supports of the gallery. But its tail glinted in the distant firelight and its smell was too strong to hide.

Alice growled, deep in her throat, and announced her presence. With a hiss the rat swung round, surprised and tense, its eyes flashing and its horrible teeth gleaming sharp and yellow in the thick light.

'Well?' Alice growled. 'Are you a friend of the Magician's?'

'I'm a friend of a magician's, yes,' the rat hissed.

'Say the password,' Alice growled.

'But not of your magician,' the rat spat. And, as it spoke it leaped clean off the stone on which it was sitting and landed on Alice's furry shoulder.

With a furious yelp, Alice turned her head, biting at the animal that was trying at the same time to bury its teeth into her flesh. She swung her body, raising both her front paws and turning a complete somersault at the same time. The rat slithered to the floor, falling on its back, but before Alice had time to spring on to it, it turned tail and fled, screaming and hissing along the length of the gallery and disappeared into a hole in the skirting.

Alice leaped at the hole, scrabbling at the wall with her huge front paws, tearing at the wood and barking ferociously.

'Spot!' she heard Mary shouting angrily from down

below in the hall. 'Alice! Can't you stop him? Phoebe's getting worse.'

'Stop now, Spot,' Alice said and, as she did so, she seemed to leap clear of the dog's body and she saw it, lying on its stomach, legs outstretched fore and aft, barking crazily at the hole in the skirting. She reached forward, putting a hand on the back of its neck, and making calming sounds.

Spot turned, mouth wide and with his tongue hanging out as he panted excitedly.

'Now do you believe me?' the voice growled in her head. 'That rat is no friend of the Magician.'

'Spot!' Alice exclaimed out loud. 'I was . . . inside you. Somehow. I was. Or it was like . . . almost as if . . . I was you. But . . . how? I don't understand.' Then she turned and leaned over the balustrade, calling excitedly, 'Oh Mary! Mary, the most incredible thing ever has just happened . . .'

But at that same moment Mary herself started to shout desperately, and so she didn't hear her sister.

'Alice. Oh, help me, somebody please. The baby, Alice. The baby is coming. Get Uncle Jack. Oh, please get somebody to help us.'

'Come on,' Spot said, scuttling down the stairs to the hall, with Alice running after him.

'But,' she shouted as she almost tripped down the stairs in her haste, 'we can't leave them, Spot. What if the rat comes back? I'm sure it means to do some harm.'

'Let it try,' an indignant voice hooted above her head, and the owl sailed down from the rafters of the hall roof, and perched on the lintel above the hearth, glaring down at them with big round eyes.

'The owl,' Mary cried, relief in her voice.

'Ooo-ooo!' the owl trilled.

'Now, owls really do scare rats,' Spot barked. 'Come on, Alice. The sooner we find Jack and William the better.'

'Will you be all right, Mare?' Alice asked, uncertain what was the wisest thing to do.

But Mary wasn't listening, she was busy getting Phoebe into a more comfortable position.

'Off you go,' the owl hooted. 'Find the fox. He'll show you the way.'

'You will look after them?' Alice called, as she followed Spot to the front door.

'Little girl,' the owl hooted, 'I eat rats for breakfast, remember? And as to delivering babies – there's nothing to it. It's as easy as laying an egg. Off with you. And travel as fast as your paws will carry you.'

Spot was waiting in the porch and then, with a mighty bound, Alice leaped out into the blizzard, as she and the dog became one again.

21

A Day We'll Remember for the Rest of Our Lives

Jack pulled himself along the ground, forcing his body to slide over the rough, uneven surface. He had managed to get hold of one straight branch. Now he needed a second to go with it. There was plenty of dead wood under the trees, but finding a sufficiently long piece was the problem. He had to move with care. If he accidently used his left leg, then a spasm of pain shot through his body which made him gasp and cry out.

But he couldn't just lie there, waiting for William to return. He felt useless and ashamed. Of all the stupid accidents: to fall and break his leg at a time like this, just when Phoebe needed him to be strong.

Reaching out with his hand he caught hold of another piece of wood and pulled it towards him. It was a bit too long, but it was the same sort of straight branch of fir as the one he had already procured. Clasping it in both his hands he broke off a piece of about equal length to the other.

Then he clamped these two bits of wood, one either

side of his injured leg, below the knee, and taking a length of string, which he had luckily found stuffed into the pocket of his anorak, he wound it round and round and tied it tightly. It was a difficult operation to accomplish in a lying position, but at least the activity got his circulation moving again. The cold, while he had been lying idle, had been so intense that he'd been afraid he was going to turn into a block of ice.

The wind still howled and rattled in the high branches above his head. He looked at his watch and saw that it was well into the afternoon. Night would be coming soon. He was desperately worried about William. The whole expedition had been foolish and dangerous. He should have known better than to set out. It would have been far wiser to have stayed at Golden House and somehow managed to deliver the baby himself. If indeed the baby was on its way. It wasn't due for three weeks. Probably the whole thing had been a false alarm.

'I'm a fool,' he shouted aloud to the silent woods. 'And I'm a fool for saying so,' he muttered, embarrassed by this useless show of emotion. 'Come on, Jack,' he told himself. 'No point in wallowing in self pity. That's not going to help anyone.'

He had already selected a branch to use as a walking stick. Now, with its aid, and grasping on to the lowest branches of a tree with his other hand, he hauled himself laboriously up into a standing position.

If he put his weight on his injured leg then the pain was unbearable but, thanks to the splint he had made for himself, he found that he could hobble slowly forward, supporting himself on his walking stick.

He decided that the best route to follow would be the path that William had taken, in the hope that he'd meet his nephew coming back. William would be certain to be looking for him, so with any luck they would find each other.

But, of course, what Jack did not know was that William was travelling with a fox and that foxes, like all wild animals, take the most direct route between two points, which often means going over ground that would be impossible for a human. Consequently Jack, following the rough track, passed the place where the fox had turned and gone downhill through the trees, and he found his way going gradually upwards instead, deeper and deeper into the forest, away from the valley road where William had found the telephone box.

William had asked to be put through to the police. He didn't want the fire brigade and an ambulance would be useless in this snow.

He explained to the man who answered that Phoebe was about to give birth to a baby at Golden House and that Jack had broken his leg while trying to get through the storm to the telephone. The policeman asked him where he was speaking from and told him to stay put until he managed to get some help through. But William knew that that could take a considerable time; although the wind was not so savage now and the snow was less blinding, it might be ages before conditions settled sufficiently for any form of rescue to be mounted. He decided to go back for Jack, in the hope that he could manage to get him down to the phone box as well. It would at least give them both some protection from the cold and it would also mean that they'd be together in an easily locatable place once the helicopter, which he was sure would be sent, could get off the ground.

The fox was waiting for him at the side of the road, its long, sleek body a dazzling red in contrast with the grey and white of the snow.

William walked towards it, extending his hand, rather as you would when approaching a dog, in a gesture of friendship. But the fox was no dog. It watched William with suspicious eyes and shied away before he got close enough to touch him.

'Here, boy!' William said, surprised by this reaction, and trying to make his voice sound enticing. He crouched in the snow, his hand still extended towards the fox, trying to coax it towards him. But the fox only slunk further away from him and then turned and scampered round behind a mound of snow that covered a low stone wall. There it paused and William could see it skulking at a distance, watching him still.

'What's the matter?' William called out. 'I thought you were my friend.'

But the fox only stared, body tense, ready to run if William made a move towards it.

'Oh, come on!' William shouted, crossly. Then, when he still got no reaction, he turned his back on the fox and looked instead at the long line of tree-covered hills where Jack was lying waiting for him.

The footprints of the fox were still just visible in a vague line, leading across the snow-covered field to a distant grey stone wall.

William remembered the sensation of flying as they leaped that wall. Then he frowned and shook his head. How could he have? The fox could have leaped the wall. But not him. And where were his footprints? True it was still snowing quite hard and they could have been covered by now but, in that case, why weren't the prints of the fox covered also?

'You really don't know, do you?' a voice in his head said.

'Know what?' William asked, aloud.

'How you got here,' the voice whispered.

'Of course I do,' William replied, feeling hot.

'Talking to yourself?' the voice in his head whispered.

William looked around uncomfortably, hoping that

no one had been listening to him. Talking to oneself was, after all, the first sign of madness.

The fox was sitting in the snow, at the side of the wall, watching him. William thought it had a rather sly expression.

'What are you waiting for, anyway?' William shouted at it.

The fox stood up on its four legs, its tail held aloft like a burning flame, and stared at him impassively.

'Well?' William demanded, feeling uncomfortable. The fox had a superior air that was most unnerving.

'Go on,' William shouted again, waving his arm. 'Go away. I thought you'd help me. Well, if you won't, just go away.'

The fox yawned, and stretched its body. The breath from its mouth smoked on the frosty air. Then it lifted its head, listening.

'Please,' William called, in a contrite voice, 'I really do need your help.'

Slowly the fox turned and looked at him. They stood staring at each other, surrounded by the vast expanse of gleaming white. The clouds were higher now and the falling snow was turning from big cotton wool blobs to a fine powder. The wind had dropped and a profound silence had settled over the countryside; that silence that only the snow brings, the sort of silence that you think you can touch, the sort of silence that clings to you and covers you and wraps itself around you.

Once again, as had happened several times recently, William felt peculiarly displaced. Perhaps it was the thick layer of snow that gave the country such a strangely anonymous blankness. Perhaps it was the extreme exertion that he had just been through that made William dizzy. Or perhaps . . .

'Perhaps it's the Magician's magic,' the fox whispered.

'You feel it too?' William asked.

'Always,' the fox replied. 'But I belong to the Magician, and not to you, little boy. I'm a wild creature. No use trying to train me like a farm dog. Understand? I hunt to survive. There's nothing soft in my life. My vixen and her cubs need me to be strong and sharp. Let me tell you, little boy, if you travel with me, it will be danger all the way.' The fox stretched again and licked its flank in a nonchalant way. Then it stared back at William with piercing eyes. 'There's a hunt round here,' it whispered.

The words made William tremble and look over his shoulder. He could feel the hair on the back of his neck stirring.

'Now?' he asked, in his head. 'Is the hunt out now?'

'No, not now,' the voice in his head continued. 'The weather's too harsh for the humans. But we have to be careful. Come on, I'm hungry. There are some hens along the way.'

As the voice spoke, William sprang forward and a moment later he could feel his paws lightly skimming across the surface of the snow.

But what about Uncle Jack? he thought.

'Can't do anything till we've eaten,' the fox told him.

William could hear the hens before he saw them. They were in a wooden house, with a wire-mesh cage in front of it. There was a gap in the wire.

'No!' William cried out, just in time. And he did so with such force that the fox sprang away from him, surprised, and somehow the two bodies became separate again.

'I couldn't eat a raw chicken,' William explained.

The fox sighed and stared at him pityingly.

'Humans!' it said in a withering voice. 'Call yourselves animals? You're neither one thing nor the other,' and without another word it squeezed under the wire and prowled towards the door of the hen house.

William backed away. He wasn't squeamish about the sight of blood. But the thought of what now was going to happen appalled him. He didn't mind hitching the odd lift with the fox, but he refused to guzzle raw chicken with it. He couldn't do that for anyone. Not even a magician.

So he turned his back and let the fox get on with it on its own.

The farmhouse was across a yard. And beside the back door leaned a sledge, half covered with snow.

William ran up to the door and banged on it with

his fist. Distantly a dog barked. But no one came to answer his calls.

He felt in his pocket to see if he had any paper and a pencil. If he had, he would leave a note explaining that he was just borrowing the sledge. But, of course, he had none.

Instead, William wrote ONLY BORROWED in the smooth snow that covered the yard and hoped that, whoever the owners of the house and the sledge were, they would get back before the snow had melted and taken his message with it.

As he passed the hen house once more, he noticed a trail of blood that led from the door of the hut, under the gap in the wire and disappeared into the undergrowth at the side of the lane.

William shuddered. He hadn't even heard a sound. He didn't like the fox much, he thought. It was a cruel creature. Then he set off up a track that led from the farm towards the tree-covered slopes, dragging the sledge behind him.

Spot raced across the snow, keeping his nose low. The scent of William and Jack wasn't very strong. It would have been easier on real earth. Ice and snow didn't hold smells satisfactorily.

'Not that we won't find them,' he assured Alice. 'But it might take a bit of time.'

Alice was enjoying the way they ploughed their nose through the loose surface of the snow and then, every so often, they would look up and shake their head and sneeze.

'It's lovely, Spot,' she told him. 'Being a dog is much much much more fun than being a girl.'

'Huh!' said Spot. 'It's not all beer and skittles, you know. Dogs have a very hard life sometimes.'

'So do girls,' Alice assured him. 'At least you don't have to sit exams and go to the dentist. And you never have to wear a skirt.' If there was one thing that Alice hated, it was wearing a skirt. She thought it the silliest invention. Boys didn't wear skirts – except in Scotland – so why should girls? However, she decided not to bother Spot with the problems of being a girl just then. They had more important things to deal with.

They reached the top of the first hill out of Golden House valley. Here the snow was so deep that Spot sank up to his chin in it and had to kick and leap his way on to a firmer surface. Then they stopped and scanned the white countryside.

The snow was also falling less thickly for them now and they were able to see miles and miles of blank white country.

'Not a sign,' Spot growled.

'The owl said we were to look for the fox,' Alice reminded him.

'Blooming owl,' Spot growled. 'Always thinks he knows what's best.'

'Why are all of you males, Spot?' Alice asked, unable to stop a complaining note from creeping into her voice. 'It really isn't fair. Why aren't any of the Magician's friends female like Mary and me?'

Spot sat back on his haunches and scratched behind his ear as he thought about this.

'I don't think the Magician has much time for women,' he said eventually.

'Huh!' said Alice furiously. But before she could speak her mind on the subject they got a faint whiff of Jack's boots striking off towards the tree line.

'They went this way,' Spot said and they bounded away, running fast towards the distant woods.

Once within their shelter the going was much easier and Spot's feet skittered across the hard earth, his nose picking up strong smells of William and Jack until, on a long straight slope, the smell of fox became over-whelming.

'Fox,' the dog growled. 'I hate fox.'

'You can't,' Alice said, surprised. 'The fox is the Magician's friend.'

'Well,' grumbled Spot, 'you don't automatically like the friends of friends, do you?'

'No,' Alice agreed, remembering one or two of Mary's friends who she thought were horrid.

They shot up the hill, following the fox's scent, until they reached a narrow track. Here, once again, they picked up the smell of William and Jack.

'The fox showed them this path,' Spot said, going slower now, much to Alice's relief. Although Spot was doing the running, she also felt as if she was using energy.

'It isn't like being on a bus, you know,' she told him.

'What isn't?' Spot demanded.

'Travelling with you. I still seem to do the moving.'

'Well of course you do,' Spot told her, as if she was really a bit thick. 'You are me and I am you.'

'Does that mean that sometimes you'll be a dog, walking about looking like a girl?' Alice asked, trying very hard to understand.

But this was too much even for Spot. He paused and scratched his ear.

'I don't know about that,' he said. 'I mean – what would be the point?'

'Well' – Alice searched for a good enough reason – 'you could come to my school or go to the cinema or for a cheeseburger or . . . things like that.'

Spot yawned and didn't even bother to reply. Alice couldn't blame him. She thought it was much more fun being a dog.

They found the place where Jack had fallen and soon after they reached where the fox and William had gone off downhill towards the valley bottom. Here they discovered Jack's scent going on alone along the forest track.

'They parted company here,' Spot said, snuffling the ground excitedly. 'And the man is only walking on one leg.'

'Only walking on one leg?' Alice said, deeply puzzled. 'How can that be?'

'He's hurt,' Spot continued, still sniffing at the ground. 'He walks heavily on one leg and trails the other. And he has a stick to support him.'

'That'll be Uncle Jack,' Alice said and then she added in a worried voice, 'Oh dear! I wonder what's happened. Which way did William go, Spot? Can you tell?'

'He's travelling with the fox, of course,' Spot replied in a matter-of-fact voice.

'You must admit all this is a bit weird,' Alice said. 'Not everyone pops in and out of animals, you know. Not everyone goes running off in a dog and sniffs things and burrows in the snow. In fact, come to think of it, I've never heard of anything like this before.'

'But then, not many people know a magician, do they?' Spot asked.

'That is very true,' Alice said, impressed by Spot's intelligence.

'Which way shall we go?' Spot asked. 'Do we follow Jack or William?'

'The owl said . . .'

'There you go again. Why does everyone pay attention to the owl?'

'The owl said . . .' Alice insisted, ignoring the dog, 'that we should find the fox.'

So saying, they hurried off the track down into the trees towards the valley bottom.

The fox finished the meal and licked his chops. Not a bad bit of chicken. Then he went to find the boy.

William hadn't got far. The sledge wasn't all that easy to pull and he was half inclined to leave it. But he reckoned that it would make transporting Jack to the road much easier once he had found him.

I hope this track leads into the right part of the woods, he thought.

'It does,' the fox told him, trotting up and walking beside him.

'Oh, it's you,' William said, surprised to hear a voice.

'Who did you think it would be?' the fox asked him, scathingly. But before William could answer him back, the sound of someone calling made them both look across the fields in the direction of the high woods.

It was a high, piping voice; a familiar voice.

'William,' it called. 'Oh, William!'

'That's Alice,' William said.

'This way,' the fox told him and the next moment

William was leaping a stone wall and streaking across the snowy ground towards the distant shape of the big black and white dog.

'Are you all right, Phoebe?' Mary asked her.

'Don't bother her with questions,' the owl told her. 'She needs all her strength.'

Mary thought the owl was rather bossy, but she was glad it was there. Twice it had flown at the rat and sent it scuttling for cover.

'I'll get it eventually,' the owl told her. 'Now what are you doing, girl?'

'I don't know,' Mary answered, desperately. 'I've never delivered a baby before.'

'Just let it come,' the owl had told her and although its voice was rather hooting and haughty, it sounded kindly.

The baby came just as the darkness settled completely round the house. It came quietly and surprisingly gently and Mary thought it was the most wonderful thing that she had ever seen anywhere or that she was ever likely to see.

'It was magic,' she told Phoebe, when she had bathed it and wrapped it in a towel and done all the other things that Phoebe instructed her to do.

'It's a boy,' Phoebe whispered, taking the baby in her arms. She wasn't really asking a question, it was more as though she was making a statement.

'No,' Mary told her, breathless still with excitement. 'It's a little girl.'

'A girl,' Phoebe said, so quietly that it was almost like a sigh.

'A girl,' the owl hooted. It was a mournful sound.

'But – isn't that good?' Mary exclaimed.

'I'm not sure,' Phoebe said.

'The Magician won't be pleased,' the owl hooted.

'But – why ever not?' Mary said. She could feel herself getting cross.

'Well,' the owl hooted. 'He was expecting a boy.'

'Well, bother the Magician,' Mary stormed. 'She's the most beautiful baby I've ever seen. She's the first baby I've ever helped be born and she's the best baby in the whole world,' and, she couldn't help it, she started to cry.

'Mary,' Phoebe whispered, holding a hand out to her. 'I agree with you. Thank you, Mary.'

'And I agree with you too,' the owl hooted. 'But I'm not sure about the Magician.'

'The Magician?' Mary said, crossly. 'Bother the Magician. She's a little girl, whether he likes it or not. And I don't see how he could fail to. Anyway, whatever the Magician says won't make any difference, because she's here.'

And, right on cue, the baby let out a great, noisy wail.

22

The Empty Room

After the blizzard died down, the clouds parted and then gradually dispersed. By nightfall, a clear sky soared, like a dark dome, over the winter landscape. Stars came out, one by one, and a thin moon floated in a halo of silver mist. The snow crunched underfoot and long thin icicles glittered like daggers from the branches of the trees and the bars of the farm gates.

Spot and the fox found Jack huddled in the shelter of a holly bush. He had lit a fire with some of the dry brushwood that lay deep in the forest, protected from the storm by the density of the trees up above. But it had given only a poor flame and little warmth and, because he found moving so difficult, he was unable to get sufficient fuel to keep it going for very long. Then, once it had died and darkness had settled over the woods, he had wrapped himself as well as he could in his anorak and, drawing his good leg up under his chin, he had prepared to sit out the night.

Eventually he fell into an uneasy sleep, full of visions and strange sounds. Later he would tell Phoebe how he had dreamed that a fox came with a dog and that they carried him to a sledge and on that he had made the journey back to Golden House.

'But, of course,' he added, 'I was dreaming. It was William and Alice who came to the rescue. Though how they managed to get through that storm beats me.'

He would remember lying on the sledge, with the dog and the fox pulling it across the sparkling, moon-lit ground.

'But as I say, it was Alice and William. How they had the strength to pull me I can't imagine.'

He would remember a sky crowded with stars like a jewel case; each one twinkling and flashing to outshine its neighbour. He would remember the sharp feeling of the icy air against his cheeks and the snow flying like a bow wave on each side of the sledge. He would remember the dark horizon, black against the blue-black of the sky, and the trees weighed down with shimmering snow, and the sound of the animals' breath as they pulled his weight, and their paws as they pounded the ground and the swish of the sledge as it skimmed across the smooth earth.

Most of all that night he would remember the sledge pausing for a moment at the summit of a hill and seeing, down below, the orange glow of lamplight spilling from the front door of Golden House, where Mary stood, impatient on the porch, waiting for his return.

Perhaps it was his fever that confused the dreams and the reality. Did a great owl swoop low over the sledge and did it call out to the dog and the fox? Or was it Mary, running out to welcome Alice and William as they pulled their heavy cargo into the drive and up the final stretch to the door?

Certainly there was a dog there. Jack remembered Alice stroking it as it lay panting at her feet. And there was a fox, which William helped to unharness from the sledge. But could that be right? Could a fox be persuaded to pull a sledge? He'd never heard of a thing like that before.

But there are many miracles and many unexplained events and sometimes it's best to leave them as precious memories in the mind and to let them, little by little, fade and alter until they become no more than fragments of a legend. And so it would be for Jack. His scientific brain couldn't wrestle for too long with the possibility of magic without him losing his trust in his own logical thinking and his reasoning capacity on which he relied almost exclusively. And this time he was saved by the greatest miracle of all.

'Uncle Jack!' Mary exclaimed, running to him. 'Oh, Uncle Jack, you're here at last. Come quickly and see.'

Phoebe was lying on the hearth rug in front of the fire, propped up on pillows and covered with blankets and an eiderdown. In her arms Jack saw that she was holding a small bundle of white towel. Then, as he hobbled towards her, leaning heavily on William, the bundle moved and turned and he was looking into the eyes of his first-born child.

'Jack,' Phoebe murmured drowsily. 'Jack, thank God you're home. She's a girl, Jack. A baby girl . . . Mary did it all . . .'

'Mare,' Alice whispered in amazement.

'It wasn't really me,' Mary whispered, blushing as she spoke. 'The owl told me what to do – and, really, babies come on their own.'

'Was it very rude?' Alice asked.

'No, of course it wasn't,' Mary assured her.

Alice had grave doubts all the same. Babies, like most other 'natural' things, were too rude to be thought about. So instead she ran out on to the porch, to look for Spot.

'Spot! Spot!' she called, finding that he and the fox had disappeared. Then she saw their footprints in the snow, leading in the direction of the trees.

'Spot!' she called again. 'Uncle Jack will let you live inside.'

Distantly she heard an answering bark, but she could see no sign of the dog and, as it was now intensely cold, she went back into the hall and closed the door.

The children helped Phoebe and Jack up the stairs to their room. Mary remade the bed and William brought them hot-water bottles. The baby was placed in a cradle beside Phoebe and she said that she would be able to manage until the morning and that they should go down into the kitchen and have some supper and then go to bed.

'You must all be tired out,' she said and indeed, as she spoke, Jack was already snoring quietly beside her.

Mary said that they could easily look after themselves and soon the three children were sitting round the kitchen range recounting all that had happened to each of them from the moment that Jack and William had set off on the journey to the phone box.

When all the stories were finished they relapsed into silence, staring at the dull embers of the fire.

'What a Christmas!' Mary said eventually. 'D'you remember Uncle Jack saying he wanted it to be a day we'd remember always?'

'Oh, Christmas!' Alice exclaimed, then she giggled.

'What d'you suppose the rat meant?' William asked. 'Tell us again what it said, Alice.'

Alice shrugged and swung her feet. It was nice being the centre of attention for once.

'He said he belonged to a magician – but not our magician.'

'Oh, no!' William groaned. 'Not two magicians!'

'You know what I think,' Mary said after a moment. 'I think the rat was trying to stop the baby being born.'

'But – why?' Alice asked.

Mary shrugged.

'Twice while the birth was taking place the owl had to scare it off.'

'Well, I told you, didn't I?' Alice said, smugly. She was really enjoying having been right about it. 'I never could bring myself to trust a rat.'

'It was the rat that destroyed the tyres,' William said. 'I suppose that was so we couldn't go for help.'

'Unless of course,' Mary pondered, 'unless this was all part of our test. The one the Magician said we should have.'

'No,' Alice protested. 'Spot asked it to say the password, and it couldn't. That rat has nothing to do with our magician, I'm sure of that.'

'What password?' William asked, filled with curiosity.

Alice shrugged.

'I don't know,' she said. 'I'll ask Spot. Oh, I really loved being in the dog. Did you, Will? Did you like being in the fox?'

'I don't know how we could have been,' William protested. 'I think it must have been some sort of a dream or something. I mean, how else can you explain it?'

Alice groaned. William was sometimes so thick.

'We don't have to explain it. Why need we? It just happened. I could smell scents and we ran through the snow with our noses so close to the ground that the snow went up our nostrils and made us sneeze.'

'Well, I nearly ate a raw chicken,' William said.

'William, you didn't?' Mary exclaimed. 'But why?'

'The fox was hungry,' William said.

'Ugh! How horrible.' Alice screwed up her face in disgust. 'It's enough to make you want to be a vegetable.'

'You are lucky,' Mary sighed. 'I didn't get to travel in anything.'

'But you delivered the baby,' Alice told her. 'You had the most important job.'

'Would you have liked it instead?' Mary asked, rather sharply.

'Not much,' Alice was forced to admit.

'Precisely. You two go off having magic and I'm left at home. Typical!' Mary filled the words with distaste.

They were silent again for a moment as each of them relived the events in their minds.

'The owl says the Magician'll be furious,' Mary said, almost to herself.

'What about?' William asked.

'The baby – being a girl,' Mary told him.

Alice nodded.

'Spot says the Magician can't be bothered with females,' she said, helping herself to another of Phoebe's mince tarts.

'Why not?' William asked.

'Because he must be a male-thingy,' Mary said. 'You know, those funny pigs.'

'A chauvinist,' William declared, solemnly.

'What are they?' Alice asked.

'They're the men that women have to fight against,' Mary told her, authoritatively.

'How d'you mean, fight against?' Alice asked, her eyes wide with excitement. 'Do we all have to?'

'It's male-thingy-pigs who have stopped women being treated as equals,' Mary told her.

'Equal to who?' Alice asked.

'Equal to men,' Mary replied, patiently.

'Ugh,' cried Alice. 'But that's stupid. Of course women aren't the same as men. I'd far rather be a man. They have a much better time. I'm sure I was meant to be a man really, only there was a mix-up at the hospital.'

'Oh, don't be silly, Alice,' Mary told her, losing her temper.

'Shut up, both of you,' William interrupted them. 'I'm thinking.'

'You see?' Mary grumbled. 'That's typical male behaviour.'

'Right,' William said, ignoring her. 'I vote we go to see the Magician.'

'Now?' Mary said.

'Why not?' William asked her. 'I won't be able to sleep until I know about the rat.'

'Oh, William,' Alice whispered. 'Will the baby be safe from the rat?'

'I don't know,' William answered her. 'That's what we need to ask the Magician.'

They hurried from the kitchen out into the hall.

The fire had crumbled to dull red ashes and the candles on the Christmas tree had guttered and were smoking.

'It looks like after a party,' Mary said, sadly. 'We never really had Christmas.'

'And we never got to eat,' Alice complained, which wasn't strictly true. She had just consumed two bowls of thick soup and a whole heap of mince pies, as William pointed out to her. 'But that doesn't count. You're supposed to have too much to eat at Christmas. Proper food: turkey and stuffing and plum pudding and trifle for supper and little sausages and sprouts – which you can leave if you don't like them which I don't – and what's that red stuff, Mare? Smoked salmon if it's sent by those people from Scotland and . . .'

'Oh, shut up, Alice,' William said, desperate to stop her. This list could go on for hours; it usually did once Alice got into full spate.

They crossed to the hearth and walked into the warm sweetly smelling, smoky chimney.

The climb to the secret room was surprisingly uneventful. Once the steps had been discovered the mystery about them ceased somehow to amaze the children. Like a short cut or a little-known path through the woods becomes quickly familiar, so now they climbed in single file to the smoke door and through it, knowing that the inner catch was the metal ring set into the wall.

Only Alice hesitated for a moment, as she remembered the rats.

'They're not there, are they?' she whispered to William, who was walking ahead of her.

'No,' he reassured her.

Then the silvery light started to filter down from the top of the steps and eventually, puffing and out of breath, they all stepped into the room.

The window-mirror at the front of the house reflected the moonlight so that the room was flooded with its thin rays.

'Hello?' William called.

But no answer came to him.

Disappointed, the three children wandered round the room, surprised at how empty and dusty it was.

'But . . .' Mary said, in a puzzled voice. 'I thought it was full of furniture and things. I'm sure I remember a chair and a table and . . .'

'Books,' Alice said, sadly. 'It was full of books, like Miss Atterton's study at school. Oh, Will – what's happened?'

William didn't know the answer any more than they did, and he felt equally disappointed.

'It's as though it never happened,' he said. 'As though we dreamed it.'

'But we didn't,' Mary protested. 'I know we didn't.'

'So – where has everything gone?' William demanded.

Then Alice, who was searching in the dark corners, in the hope of finding some clue to what was going on, let out a cry of surprise.

'What is it?' William and Mary said in unison, running to join her.

'Oh, look!' their younger sister cried.

She was pointing at a circular mirror, hanging on the wall, its frame made of dark wood.

'It's just a looking glass, Alice,' William said, and then he was surprised that he should have chosen such an old-fashioned word. Why not 'mirror'? he thought.

'Yes, but – don't you see?' Alice insisted.

Mary stared at the glass, puzzled. There was something funny about it, Alice was right. And then she also realized.

'Oh!' Mary cried.

'What?' William sounded impatient.

He walked up to the mirror, which was hanging at an angle above his head, and stared into it.

No reflection stared back.

William waved his hand.

No answering wave showed on the mirror's surface.

'We aren't there,' he said.

They peered in puzzlement at the scene through the glass. It was so dark and dusty that it was almost impossible to see anything at all. But gradually images began to form of the room in which they were standing. But the room looked totally different because it was furnished.

Mary looked over her shoulder, to be sure that the room hadn't somehow changed. But it was empty and dusty and dark. She looked back at the scene through the mirror.

A fire was burning in a grate.

'There isn't a grate,' Mary said to herself.

'Yes,' Alice told her. 'Over here,' and she ran to show them a small stone hearth, empty and cold.

They looked again into the mirror.

'What does it mean?' William asked.

They frowned and pondered and were silent.

'We'll have to ask the owl,' Mary said at last.

'Or the fox,' William said.

'Spot will know,' Alice said, to herself.

'But even the animals have gone away,' Mary said. 'In fact, if there isn't a baby sleeping beside Phoebe's bed, I shall really think that we dreamed it all.'

'Oh,' Alice sighed, and she felt a lump forming in her throat. 'I don't want it all to have been a dream. That's why I hated *Alice in Wonderland*. It's such a cheat if it's all a dream. Oh, please, Mr Magician. Come back. Please!'

In the mirror, the fire in the hearth flared up and then

a shadow seemed to cross the mirror as though someone was looking into it from the other side. Some unseen
face was staring at them through the round frame.

'D'you feel that?' William asked, speaking all their
thoughts.

The girls didn't reply, but they seemed to agree. All
three of them knew that in some strange way they were
being looked at through the mirror and that they were as
surprising to the mysterious viewer as the furnished room
and the fire was to them.

'What's happening?' William asked, trying not to panic.

'I think we're being tested,' Mary said.

'But I thought . . . wasn't everything that's happened
the test?' William argued.

Mary shook her head, solemnly.

'I think we were supposed to be tested in order that
we could do what we have already done. I think that
the time has got muddled up.'

'I don't understand,' William said in despair. He
couldn't bear not understanding.

'Neither do I, really,' Mary said, wearily.

'Well, who can tell us, then?' William demanded.

'The Magician?' Mary suggested, tentatively.

'But the rat said there was another magician. His
magician,' Alice said. 'A bad magician. I think he's looking at us now. I feel all goose-pimply – like when the
rats came. William! Mary!'

They turned and looked at her.

'Let's go to bed,' she whispered.

'You're probably right,' William said. 'We can't work this out on our own. The Magician must help us or we won't be able to help him, which is what he said he wants. Well I'm sick of trying to work things out on our own. Come on. I agree with Alice. I'm tired. I want to go to bed.'

And so saying, William turned and walked back towards the door in the chimney.

'But won't we ever see the Magician again?' Alice asked, sadly.

'I'm sure we will – when he needs us,' William replied.

'Don't we have any say?' Mary asked, crossly. 'That's so typical of a man. Expecting us to hang about waiting on his beck and call – whatever that is!'

'I know,' William agreed. 'But then, I don't know what I'd ask him if I saw him.'

'I do,' Mary said, sadly. 'I'd like to have gone in an animal like both of you did. I mean, if I'm honest, it was incredibly interesting and all that when the baby was born. But it wasn't exactly magic, was it? I'd like to have travelled with the fox or with the dog. Or,' she ended, wistfully, 'maybe I could have flown with the owl.'

'Oh, well,' a voice hooted over her head, 'if that's all you wanted, you should have asked. Come on. No time like the present.'

The owl was sitting on his perch with the round window open in front of him. Outside, the crisp winter night was full of wind and stars and animals.

'William,' Mary called, fearfully.

But even as she spoke, it was too late. The owl stood up, staring at her. Then, spreading her wings, Mary launched herself off the perch and through the opening, out into the dark.

23

The Return of the Magician

Mary opened her eyes with a start. The room was full of light, but it wasn't this that had woken her. There was a strange noise, a throbbing, beating, swishing sort of sound, and it was coming from outside the window.

She sat up and shivered. It was very cold in the room. Alice's bed was empty, and the door was wide open on to the landing.

She got up quickly and scrambled into a pair of jeans and a thick sweater. Then she pulled on some woollen socks.

The sound she could hear was a machine. But what kind of machine? She crossed to the window and peered out. Whatever it was was not in view from the bedroom window. She shivered again and ran a hand through her hair. As she did so a white feather, caught in her hair the previous night, floated down in front of her face and landed on the floor.

At once she remembered her dream. She had been flying, out in the night. She remembered the feeling of icy wind on her arms and the view of the snow-covered ground over which she had sailed. The tops of trees came into the picture: firs, rising to needle points tipped with snow, and the big leafless oaks and ashes all a jumble of branches and twigs, which held pockets of snow and were suspended with glittering icicles.

Then she saw the mouse. It was no more than a tiny dot on the white ground. It was searching for food, she supposed. Going about its business, doing no one any harm. From a great height, Mary fell through the crackling night. The wind whistled in her ears and tiny particles of frozen air settled on her cheeks. At the last moment before hitting the ground, she turned her body and saw her great talons reaching out and grabbing the tiny creature up from the snow. It screamed once, a minute gasp of terror. Then Mary carried its limp body beneath her to the ledge of the dovecot, where she settled and started to tear its body with her beak . . .

Mary sat down, with a gasp, on the side of the bed. She covered her eyes with her hands, trying to blot out the picture that her memory was recreating. She could even taste the blood . . .

Rising quickly, she ran to the bathroom and was sick into the lavatory. Then she knelt on the floor and started to cry.

Later William came to her, breathless with running. 'Come on, Mare!' he said. 'The doctor wants to meet you,' and he ran out again, back down the narrow stone steps, without even noticing that she had been crying.

Mary splashed cold water on her face and dried herself on a towel. Then she hurried down into the hall. The front door was open and she could hear voices coming from outside. She crossed to it and went out on to the porch.

A helicopter was standing on the lawn, with its engine switched off. Jack was being helped aboard by the pilot. William and Alice were standing watching and there was a man whom Mary didn't recognize, standing with them. As she stepped out of the porch this man turned and looked at her.

'So this is the young lady, is it?' he said to William, as he walked towards her.

'Oh, yes,' William replied. 'This is my sister, Mary.'

'And it is you who delivered the baby?' the man asked.

'Well, I helped a bit,' Mary replied, feeling her cheeks turning to scarlet.

'Congratulations,' the man said. 'If you ever think about becoming a nurse, I'm sure you'd stand a good chance of making a fine one.'

'No, I'd rather be a doctor, I think,' Mary replied.

Actually, she'd never thought about being a doctor. But the man seemed to suggest that nursing was a good job for women – he had a distinctly sexist look about him.

'Well, if you're going to be a doctor, I'd better look to my laurels,' he replied with a grin. 'You'll do me out of a job in no time.'

'Where's Uncle Jack going?'

'I have to set that leg,' the doctor explained. 'I can do it here – but I'll do a better job at the hospital. We'll get him back by nightfall. And with a few provisions for you. It'll be a day or two before they get the roads open.' The doctor turned to William. 'Now, you'll be all right, won't you? Your aunt will be here with you. I would have taken her and the child in as well. But she's a very stubborn woman.' He looked at the surrounding countryside. 'What possesses people to tuck themselves away in such remote areas, I never can fathom. Though I dare say this place has its enchantment. Keep the mother and the baby warm and no harm will come to them.'

Then he said goodbye to them and crunched across the hard snow to the helicopter. Once he was aboard, the blades started to turn, slowly at first and then faster until it seemed to be going backwards and the air from it raised the loose snow in a cloud off the ground.

As it rose into the air, the children saw Jack waving to them from a window. Mary looked away, fighting back the memories of flying and the terrible nausea that accompanied them.

Eventually the clattering noise died away and they

were left, standing on the white lawn, with their backs to the house, facing the great bank of trees.

The Magician was standing in the shelter of a spreading yew, leaning heavily on his silver rod, staring at them.

Later Mary would recall how, for a moment, it was as though they could see him and he couldn't see them.

He was wearing a long black cloak and his thin fuzz of red hair moved in the breeze left by the helicopter.

Alice was the first to speak.

'There he is!' she cried, in a delighted voice.

Maybe she saw him a moment before the others; later none of them could be sure. What is certain is that her voice, breaking the silence, seemed also to start the ensuing scene.

'There you are,' he said. 'What a lot of trouble you've caused. I can't stay long. Now what is it you want?'

The children were rather surprised by this speech. It seemed to suggest that they had summoned the Magician, which wasn't true at all.

'Well? Well?' he said, impatiently. 'Hurry up. It's taken me years to learn how to materialize like this; and the concentration is very demanding. It is particularly difficult out of doors. Tell me about the baby.'

'It's a girl.' Mary was surprised at how loud her voice sounded.

'So I believe. Jasper told me. Jasper was responsible for the birth.'

William frowned.

'Who's Jasper?' he asked.

'The owl is called Jasper. The fox is called Cinnabar. The dog . . .'

'The dog,' Alice interrupted him hurriedly, 'is called Spot.'

The Magician looked at her and frowned. It was a fierce face, but Alice was determined not to show if she was frightened, which needless to say, she was.

There was a moment of terrible silence. Then the Magician continued speaking.

'And the dog is called Spot,' he said.

'Well,' William said, 'Jasper didn't get it quite right. It was Mary who delivered the baby.'

'No, Will,' Mary stepped towards him, 'the owl helped.'

'I haven't got time for this bickering,' the Magician snapped. 'Now listen to me carefully. I had naturally hoped for a man child in your age. I find women difficult to train. You can't have a woman magician, their minds are too engrossed. They see the problems. They make good witches. But I didn't want a witch in your time. Obviously the mother got it wrong. There have been far too many women Tylers. The father is a Green. He should have known better. And, as for you three! Constants used to be reliable. My best assistant was a Constant. Matthew Constant. He was killed in a riding accident. I had to replace him with Morden. Morden is my assistant now.

Beware of Morden. He knows too much. He's bright –
but he works for himself. I should stop him. But I need
him. He has acquired many of the arts. I thought he was
conscientious. I thought that was why he worked so late
and so long. But he is greedy. Beware the greedy. They
would make gold. You understand?'

The Magician turned and walked towards the trees.
The breeze caught the folds of his cloak and the sun, as
it broke through the clouds, shone round him like a halo
of light.

'But did you notice,' Mary would tell them later, 'he
had no shadow? The sun was shining, but he cast no
shadow on the earth.'

Then the Magician turned and spoke to them again.

'The baby will be vulnerable, until I can start to teach
her. I am entrusting her into the guardianship of you three
Constant children. When you are not here then it will be
up to you to instruct Jasper and Cinnabar and . . .'

'Spot,' Alice prompted him.

'Spot,' the Magician repeated, with a certain distaste
in his voice. Then he sighed. 'Does it have to be Spot?'

Alice nodded firmly.

'Very well,' he sighed again. 'Spot! You must instruct
them to look after the family for you,' he continued.
'The father, Green – your uncle – must be handled with
care. He also is a magician of a sort – but one of your
modern ones. What is it you call us now? A scientist?

Poor language! What have you done to it? It has no poetry in it. Ah well. That isn't my job at the moment. What was I talking about? Oh, yes. Your uncle – he has some good ideas. But first he must unlearn a great deal . . . The mother, being a Tyler, naturally understands, but without really knowing very much – if indeed she knows anything at all. She's like a person who knows that she's been dreaming, but can't quite remember the content of the dream. She may learn, I suppose. That's why I gave her the talisman, in the hope that it would help her to recall . . .'

'He must mean the pendant Uncle Jack found, and gave to Phoebe for Christmas,' Mary whispered.

'Be quiet!' the Magician snapped, making Mary jump back and then pout. 'Right,' he said, looking up at the sun, 'time to be off. Ask questions.'

The three children looked at each other.

'Can we really live in animals?' Alice asked.

'Not exactly, no. You can experience them and they can carry you with them. But you couldn't become one of them. It would be a form of blasphemy to change the nature of things. That we would never allow. Besides, what would be the point? It would serve no useful purpose, becoming an animal. Or a bird,' he added, as if it were an afterthought. 'Or a fish,' he continued. 'Why not? A fish might be a useful experience.' He turned once more and stared at them with flashing eyes.

'Remember always that the creatures are here to serve you. But be very careful; remember also that you are here to serve them. The day man first believed he was superior to the animal kingdom, that day the slow decline began. For you it is now very late. Your world is dying around you. My world. My future. All that we have striven for; the few of us who saw and knew and understood the signs. Am I too late? I don't know. That is why I have had to project myself forward in time to your age. From one Elizabethan age to the next. From light to dark. From the high hope of the Renaissance to the high hope of the age of space.'

This long speech ended with the Magician mumbling to himself and shaking his head. Once again it seemed almost as though the children had ceased to exist for him; that he couldn't see them, or rather that they were not part of his world.

'Please,' William asked. 'When you're not here with us – where do you go?'

'Oh, dear. That is a very difficult question. I can't actually claim ever to "be here" with you. No, not that. I'm not living here. I am projecting myself here. Do you understand?'

'Like television?' Mary asked, hazarding an inspired guess.

'Very good,' the Magician cried. 'Precisely!' Then he frowned. 'What is – television?'

'They don't have one here,' Alice said in a subdued voice. 'Otherwise we could show you.'

'Explain to me,' the Magician snapped. 'What is this . . . television?'

'Oh, sausages!' Alice sighed. 'It'd be very hard to explain. You have this box, and when you switch it on, you get pictures.'

'You get paintings?'

'No.' Alice shook her head. 'Moving pictures. I mean – d'you know what a film is?'

'A film of oil on water?' the Magician asked.

'No!' Alice laughed. 'A film – you know. Like *ET* or *Indiana Jones* . . . A film?' she ended on a hopeful note.

'Indiana who?' the Magician demanded.

'William – you try,' Alice said, retiring from the debate.

'I can't,' William protested. 'It's quite complicated really.'

'So is projecting oneself forward in time,' the Magician agreed. 'Suffice to accept that you can see me. All right? Now, if you'll excuse me. I am expecting company tonight.'

'Where?'

'At home,' the Magician replied.

'But – where is your home?'

'Here – at Gelden House,' the Magician replied.

'Is it Christmas with you?' William asked him.

'Naturally – oh dear, I do see that it is complicated

for you. It is *time* of course that is the culprit, because it doesn't really exist. Time is just a thin . . . film perhaps? . . . a layer . . . Yes, that's it. A layer. We simply belong to different layers, that's all. Now do you understand?'

But he had only to look at their faces to know that they didn't.

'No. Not many of my pupils do, at first. But we must persevere,' he declared.

'Are you a schoolteacher?' Alice asked, hearing him mention his pupils.

'Not exactly, no. But, of course, we must pass on all that we learn. Knowledge that dies with us is dead knowledge. It benefits no one.'

'Will we ever come back to your time?' Mary asked him.

'Possibly. But we must be very sure that you know how to get back to here again. Oh, you have a lot to experience. A lot to do. It is absolutely essential that the Tyler baby is prepared for the great work. I suppose a woman will be able to manage it. But it's very different in my day.'

'You've got a woman on the throne, though,' Mary couldn't resist pointing out.

'True,' the Magician replied. 'And a deal of trouble she gives us all. They have to be flattered all the time.'

'What about her father? I bet you had to flatter Henry the Eighth even more,' Mary said.

'That is very true. Those were not particularly auspicious times. It is certainly better now, with Bess on the throne. She's actually quite keen on the alchemical arts, though of course she doesn't like her subjects to know.' The Magician nodded at her and smiled. 'You are very wise. Have you been to my time, little girl?'

Mary blushed and shook her head.

'She's awfully good at history,' Alice explained in a bored voice.

'History? Am I history to you? How very odd. And you are the future to me. I tell you, magic startles me sometimes. Now, heigh ho! And no more questions, or I shall want to sleep all through the company.'

And turning his back on them, he marched towards the snow-covered hillside.

'Wait!' William called urgently.

'Now what?' the Magician asked, crossly.

'The rat. Is the rat part of your plan?'

'The rat?' the Magician asked, surprised. 'I don't care for rats. The house is overrun with them. Morden has been doing experiments with rats. The rat will be Morden's creature.'

'We think the rat tried to prevent the baby being born.'

'That's more than likely,' the Magician replied, sounding unconcerned. 'Morden has followed me here before. I suspect he finds your world very much to his liking.

Morden also is only interested in gold. Yes, he wouldn't want me alive in your time. Morden would want your time to himself. It's a pity really I took him on, but – he's very good at the job. I knew at the time he would try to destroy me. What I didn't realize was that he had his mind set on your acquisitive age. But really,' he added as an afterthought, 'I should have thought of that for myself!'

'But, what shall we do?' William was desperate.

'Do?' the Magician asked. 'What should you do? Well, if you're no match for Morden, you're no match for anyone.'

'Is this our test?' Mary asked.

'All life's a test,' the Magician replied, 'or so I have found. Did I say I'd set you a test? Oh, well, I expect you've passed. I need you, so I can't exactly afford to fail you, can I? You'll do. You'll do very well. Constant was my best assistant. Now I really must say farewell. The creatures will be a great boon to you. Happy the day I first projected into the owl. Not this owl, of course. Or is it perhaps this owl? I get so confused. Really, magic is very puzzling . . .'

'If we need to see you . . .' William called after him.

'Then I'm sure that you'll find me. But I expect you'll manage very well on your own. The three of you. Two girls and a boy. Of course in my time we keep our girls at home. Customs obviously change most significantly after my death. Fascinating, really. Things never quite work out the way one expects them to . . .'

And, still chattering away to himself, and without looking back, the Magician walked into the deep forest and disappeared from view.

'He's gone,' Alice said sadly.

Then Phoebe's voice prevented any further discussion.

'Children,' she called, from the house. 'I've been watching you all standing there in a dream! Come inside. It's far too cold to play out there.'

'Play!' William said, scornfully.

But Mary smiled.

'I think it's rather sweet, really.'

'What, Mare?' Alice asked.

'How little grown-ups really know,' Mary replied.

And fortified with this reassuring observation the children went back into the house.

24

A Naming

The snow started to thaw three days later and by the time the children were due to leave Golden House it was sliding off the steep roofs in wedges and falling to the ground with wet thuds. Everywhere was dripping with water as the icicles melted and the trees released the captive snow. Soon stones started to show through the rough snow on the drive and a few blades of long grass forced their way through the slushy surface of the lawn.

On the night before the children's departure Phoebe cooked a special meal for them all to make up for having missed Christmas.

Jack's leg was still in plaster and he had to hobble about with the help of a crutch.

William spent the last day getting a whole stack of logs into the house and Alice and Mary tied up bunches of twigs for kindling and laid the bundles in the dry. They were concerned that the house should be kept warm for the baby and they knew that Jack would find these jobs difficult to do on his own until the plaster was removed from his leg.

On an earlier day William had walked all the way to the moor road and found the farmhouse from which he had borrowed the sledge. He returned it to the farmer's wife, who insisted on his having tea and waiting for her husband to return from milking. Then the farmer drove him back along the snow-packed lanes to Golden House on the back of his tractor.

The farmer, whose name was Mr Jenkins, was introduced to Jack and Phoebe and he told them that if they needed anything at all, they had only to ask.

'There is one thing,' Jack said, looking a little embarrassed to be taking up this kind offer so quickly.

'Just ask,' Mr Jenkins said. 'If I haven't got it, then you can't have it!'

'No, it's . . . because of my stupid leg, I won't be able to drive the children to Druce Coven Halt . . .'

'Good gracious now,' the farmer said with a smile. 'Tell me the time, tell me the day and keep your eyes open. I'll be here. It'd be a pleasure.'

So it had been arranged that Mr Jenkins would call for them at nine o'clock on the morning of their departure.

Now, as the night drew in, stuffed full of Phoebe's leek and lentil tart, followed by chocolate mousse, they all sat for the last time in front of a roaring fire in the hall of Golden House.

Phoebe was holding the baby, fast asleep, on her lap

and Jack had his plastered leg propped up on a footstool in front of him.

The children stared into the flames of the fire and watched the sparks from the burning logs leap and dance up the dark cavern of the chimney.

It was a quiet, relaxing time and they would probably have nodded off to sleep if a sudden, impatient barking hadn't sent Alice running to the front door.

'Come in, Spot,' she said, opening it wide, and the big black and white dog trotted into the hall and over to the fire.

Here he paused and looked up at Jack, expectantly.

'What d'you want, eh?' Jack asked him, leaning forward and holding his hand to the dog's nose. 'What is it, Spot?'

'He wants you to say he can stay, Uncle Jack,' Alice told him.

'I thought that had been decided,' Jack said with a smile.

'By all of us, yes,' Phoebe said. 'But he wants to hear it from you, Jack.'

'Please, Uncle Jack,' Alice implored. 'You'll never regret it. He'll be the best house dog.' As she spoke she glanced at her brother and sister, trying to get them to side with her.

'It's true,' William said. 'This is a lonely place. And when you're away, Phoebe will be glad of the dog's company.'

'And protection,' Alice added.

'And the baby,' Mary said. 'The dog will guard the baby.'

'Now what does the baby need guarding from?' Jack teased them.

'You never know,' Alice said, feeling desperate. 'I'm right, aren't I, Phoebe?'

'She is, Jack,' Phoebe said, quietly. 'They all are. Just look at him. He looks as if he belongs here and well, there is a rat about somewhere. I told you I could hear one. Well, I was right. We saw it, didn't we, Mary?'

'Yes,' Mary said, shuddering as she remembered.

'A dog would soon frighten that old rat away . . .'

'I give in! I give in!' Jack said, laughing, then, very formally, he turned to Spot and said: 'Spot, would you like to come and live with us in Golden House?'

The dog's excited barking woke the baby, but no one minded.

'Now, children,' Phoebe said, as she rocked her in her arms, 'Jack and I have decided to ask you if you will be the godparents of the baby. We can't think of anyone we would rather have to look after her and what is more, we want you to decide on her name.'

'But – haven't you thought of one already?' Mary cried, surprised by this request.

'We always said the baby would tell us,' Jack told them with a laugh. 'But she doesn't seem to say much yet.'

'If she had been a boy, we were going to call him Stephen,' Phoebe said. 'I don't know why exactly. We just liked the name. But we never thought she'd be a girl.'

'Stephanie,' William said, without hesitation. 'Stephanie Tyler.'

'Taylor,' Phoebe corrected him. Then she said thoughtfully: 'Stephanie. Stephanie Taylor. That's nice, Jack. What d'you think?'

'I like it,' Jack replied. And so it was agreed.

Stephanie meanwhile sighed in her sleep as if to say that she was pleased with the decision. And the children hoped that Stephen Tyler, who even now might be sitting beside the same fire that was warming them, in the distant past where he belonged, would approve of the name also.

Spot stretched out in the warmth with a contented yawn and distantly, outside the windows, an owl hooted in the night and a sharp, staccato barking reminded them all of the wild presence of a fox.

'Listen to them,' Phoebe whispered to the baby. 'All the creatures are saying hello, Stephanie. Do you hear that?'

And the infant kicked her legs and reached up a tiny hand and touched her mother's face.

Eventually it was time for bed. Alice was already half asleep and Mary and William had to help her up the stairs.

'Good night,' their uncle called to them.

'Good night,' Phoebe whispered.

'Good night,' they said in return.

But Spot didn't say anything. He was asleep already.

A pale watery sun shone from an almost cloudless sky. Everywhere was filled with the sound of running water as the brooks and the ditches filled up with the snow melt.

Mr Jenkins arrived punctually at nine and the children bade farewell to Jack and Phoebe and to Stephanie and Spot.

'But not for long,' Jack called to them, as they clambered up on to the trailer that Mr Jenkins had hitched to his Land-Rover and in which, after a lot of pleading, Phoebe had said it would be all right for them to travel.

They drove slowly away from Golden House, while Jack and Phoebe stood in the porch, waving them out of sight. Then they wound up the steep hill towards the moor road. The sides of the drive were still piled high with snow and the distant tree-covered woods were black and white against the blue sky, like a drawing that was just beginning to be coloured.

At one moment Mr Jenkins stopped and leaned out of the window, calling to them:

'Fox! Can you see him?' and he pointed up through the trees to where a smudge of red lurked behind a trunk, watching. 'Dratted creature,' Mr Jenkins shouted.

'I'll get you. He's had half my chickens this winter, blooming thing!'

William turned as the Land-Rover drove on, watching the bright eyes. He lifted his hand in a small gesture of friendship.

'Go carefully,' he whispered. 'Be safe.'

Then, realizing that Mary and Alice were watching him, he stuffed his hands into his pockets and looked embarrassed.

'Well,' he said with a shrug, 'foxes have to live, like everyone else. I mean, what's the farmer got chickens in a hut for in the first place? He's going to eat them, isn't he? It's either him or the fox.'

'Poor chickens,' Mary said, fighting back tears. She was remembering the owl and the taste of the blood. I think, maybe, I'll be a vegetarian, she thought. Phoebe can give me recipes.

'Wasn't it all wonderful?' Alice said quietly. 'I don't think anyone would ever believe how wonderful it's all been.'

'I don't think we should tell anyone,' William said.

And so they agreed to keep it a secret between the three of them.

'Solemn honour,' they said in unison, as they clasped hands.

'And this time, William,' Mary said in a threatening voice, 'you're not to go breaking the vow.'

'Oh,' William groaned, 'aren't you ever going to forget about that?'

'When we get to Bristol, Mare,' Alice interrupted them, 'do we have any time before our next train?'

'Half an hour, I think,' Mary replied.

'I shall have three sausages in the snack bar,' Alice said contentedly.

Then they all fell silent once more and watched as Golden Valley receded into the glimmering distance and with it the magic and danger and the friends they had made there.

'Won't be long till the spring holidays,' William said.

The Door in the Tree

Book II of The Magician's House

Alice was lost.

'William!' she called, fighting back the panic that she could feel welling up from her stomach, making her heart beat faster and a lump of tears form in the back of her throat.

'William? Mary?' she shouted, louder this time. Then she paused, waiting, without much hope, for an answering call.

The silence that surrounded her was almost throbbing. It seemed solid, like the great circle of trees that hemmed her in. She shouted again, but . . .

When Alice gets lost in the forest behind Golden House a new adventure starts for the three children which brings them into contact with the horrifying cruelty of badger baiting and makes them each prove their courage in a way that they would not have believed possible before. Is it all part of the Magician's plan for them? Or does even he abandon them? Who is the strange woman who lives on the heights above the valley? And what are the secrets they will discover beyond THE DOOR IN THE TREE?

THE DOOR IN THE TREE, Book II of The Magician's House, is available in Red Fox paperback.